His eyes ... if he was ... memory.

... ...kbeat of ... her blood ... His eyes ...pped to her mouth, pausing there for an infinitesimal moment.

'In another life I would've kissed you the other night,' he said in a gravel-rough tone. 'I probably would've taken you to bed as well.'

Molly looked at his mouth. She could see the tiny vertical lines of his lower lip and the slight dryness that she knew would cling to her softer one like sandpaper on silk. 'Why not in this life?' she asked softly.

He reached out and br... the pad of his index ... light as a moth's wing ... bubbly, tingly sensatio...

'I think you know why not,' he said, and stepped back from her.

Molly felt as if the floor of her stomach had dropped right out of her as he turned and left the room. She put her hand to her mouth, touching where his finger had so briefly been...

Dear Reader

Every day the news is full of stories of tragic events—bad things happening to good people. I often wonder what happens to those *other* victims. The ones left behind to cope in whatever way they can with what happened.

That is the essence of Lucas and Molly's story. Lucas is a man in need of redemption. He has spent seventeen years paying for the accidental death of Matt Drummond, Molly's older brother and his best mate since childhood. A workaholic who has virtually no private life, Lucas is locked down emotionally and deeply lonely and isolated—although he would never admit that to anyone!

When Molly turns up at his London hospital for a short-term appointment he is determined to keep her at arm's length. But when Molly's landlord threatens to evict her after she rescues a stray cat, Lucas steps in and offers to share his big old empty house with her. While Lucas is confident he can remain professional and distant with her at work, living under the same roof as Molly soon stirs up a blistering passion between them!

But the past is a wound that has never quite healed. Lucas is still struggling to come to terms with his role in the accident that took his best friend's life. How can he be with Molly when he is the person responsible for causing her and her family such heartache?

Lucas and Molly are two of my favourite characters. Yes, I know—I say that about every hero and heroine. Molly is caring and kind, compassionate and giving—the perfect partner for a man who has taught himself not to love.

Their story is one of redemption and the healing power of love. I hope you enjoy following them on their journey to the happy-ever-after they both deserve so much.

Warmest wishes

Melanie Milburne

THEIR MOST FORBIDDEN FLING

BY
MELANIE MILBURNE

To Tony and Jacqui Patiniotis and their sons, Lucien,
Julius and Raphael, for their generous support to the
National Heart Foundation in Hobart. This one is for you!

First published in Great Britain 2013
by Mills & Boon, an imprint of Harlequin (UK) Limited.
Harlequin (UK) Limited, Eton House,
18-24 Paradise Road, Richmond, Surrey TW9 1SR

© Melanie Milburne 2013

ISBN: 978 0 263 89888 0

Printed and bound in Spain
by Blackprint CPI, Barcelona

From as soon as **Melanie Milburne** could pick up a pen she knew she wanted to write. It was when she picked up her first Harlequin Mills & Boon at seventeen that she realised she wanted to write romance. Distracted for a few years by meeting and marrying her own handsome hero, surgeon husband Steve, and having their two boys, plus completing a Masters of Education and becoming a nationally ranked athlete (masters swimming) she decided to write. Five submissions later she sold her first book and is now a multi-published, award-winning *USA TODAY* bestselling author. In 2008 she won the Australian Readers Association's most popular category/series romance, and in 2011 she won the prestigious Romance Writers of Australia R*BY award.

Melanie loves to hear from her readers via her website, www.melaniemilburne.com.au, or on Facebook: http://www.facebook.com/pages/Melanie-Milburne/351594482609

Recent titles by Melanie Milburne:

DR CHANDLER'S SLEEPING BEAUTY
SYDNEY HARBOUR HOSPITAL: LEXI'S SECRET*
THE SURGEON SHE NEVER FORGOT
THE MAN WITH THE LOCKED AWAY HEART

Sydney Harbour Hospital

**These books are also available in eBook format
from www.millsandboon.co.uk**

CHAPTER ONE

MOLLY SAW HIM first. He was coming out of a convenience store half a block from her newly rented bedsit. He had his head down against the sleeting rain, his forehead knotted in a frown of concentration. Her heart gave a dislocated stumble as he strode towards her. The memories came rushing back, tumbling over themselves like clothes spinning in a dryer. She didn't even realise she had spoken his name out loud until she heard the thready sound of her voice. 'Lucas?'

He stopped like a puppet suddenly pulled back on its strings. The jolt of recognition on his face was painful to watch. She saw the way his hazel eyes flinched; saw too the way his jaw worked in that immeasurable pause before he spoke her name. 'Molly...'

It had been ten years since she had heard his voice. A decade of living in London had softened his Australian outback drawl to a mellifluous baritone that for some reason sent an involuntary shiver over her skin. She looked at his face, drinking in his features one by one as if ticking off a checklist inside her head to make sure it really was him.

The landscape of his face—the brooding brow, the determined jaw and the aquiline nose—was achingly familiar and yet different. He was older around the eyes and mouth, and his dark brown hair, though thick and glossy, had a few streaks of silver in it around his temples. His skin wasn't quite as weathered and tanned as his father's or brothers' back on the farm at home, but it still had a deep olive tone.

He was still imposingly tall and whipcord lean and fit, as if strenuous exercise was far more important to him than rest and relaxation. She looked at his hazel eyes. The same shadows were there—long, dark shadows that anchored him to the past.

'I was wondering when I'd run into you,' Molly said to fill the bruised silence. 'I suppose Neil or Ian told you I was coming over to work at St Patrick's for three months?'

His expression became inscrutable and closed. 'They mentioned something about you following a boyfriend across,' he said.

Molly felt a blush steal over her cheeks. She still wasn't quite sure how to describe her relationship with Simon Westbury. For years they had been just friends, but ever since Simon had broken up with his long-term girlfriend Serena, they had drifted into an informal arrangement that was convenient but perhaps not as emotionally satisfying as Molly would have wished. 'Simon and I have been out a couple of times but nothing serious,' she said. 'He's doing a plastics registrar year over here. I thought it'd be good to have someone to travel with since it's my first time overseas.'

'Where are you staying?' Lucas asked.

'In that house over there,' Molly said, pointing to a seen-better-days Victorian mansion that was divided into small flats and bedsits. 'I wanted somewhere within walking distance of the hospital. Apparently lots of staff from abroad set up camp there.'

He acknowledged that with a slight nod.

Another silence chugged past.

Molly shifted her weight from foot to foot, the fingers of her right hand fiddling with the strap of her handbag where it was slung over her shoulder. 'Um… Mum said to say hello…'

His brows gave a micro-lift above his green and brown-flecked eyes but whether it was because of cynicism, doubt or wariness, she couldn't quite tell. 'Did she?' he asked.

Molly looked away for a moment, her gaze taking in the gloomy clouds that were suspended above the rooftops of the row of grey stone buildings. It was so different from the expansive skies and blindingly bright sunshine of the outback back home. 'I guess you heard my father's remarried…' She brought her gaze back up when he didn't respond. 'His new wife Crystal is pregnant. The baby's due in a couple of months.'

His eyes studied her for a beat or two. 'How do you feel about having a half-sibling?'

Molly pasted on a bright smile. 'I'm thrilled for them… It will be good to have someone to spoil. I love babies. I'll probably babysit now and then for them when I get back…'

He continued to look at her in that measured way of his. Could he see how deeply hurt she was that her father was trying to replace Matt? Could he see how guilty she felt about *feeling* hurt? Matt had been the golden child, the firstborn and heir. Molly had lived in his shadow for as long as she could remember—never feeling good enough, bright enough.

Loved enough.

With a new child to replace the one he had lost, her father would have no need of her now.

'You're a long way from home,' Lucas said.

Did he think she wasn't up to the task? Did he still see her as that gangly, freckle-faced kid who had followed him about like a devoted puppy? 'I'm sure I'll cope with it,' she said with the tiniest elevation of her chin. 'I'm not a little kid any longer. I'm all grown up now in case you hadn't noticed.'

His gaze moved over her in a thoroughly male appraisal that made Molly's spine suddenly feel hot and tingly. As his eyes re-engaged with hers the air tightened, as if a light but unmistakable current of electricity was pulsing through it. 'Indeed you are,' he said.

Molly glanced at his mouth. He had a beautiful mouth, one that implied sensuality in its every line and contour. The shadow of dark stubble surrounding it gave him an intensely male look that she found captivating. She wondered when that mouth had last smiled. She wondered when it had last kissed someone.

She wondered what it would feel like to be kissed by him.

Molly forced her gaze to reconnect with his. She needed to get her professional cap on and keep it on. They would be working together in the same unit. No one over here needed to know about the tragic tie that bound them so closely. 'Well, then,' she said, shuffling her feet again. 'I guess I'll see you at the hospital.'

'Yes.'

She gave him another tight, formal smile and made to move past but she had only gone a couple of paces when he said her name again. 'Molly?'

Molly slowly turned and looked at him. The lines about his mouth seemed to have deepened in the short time she had been talking to him. 'Yes?' she said.

'You might not have been informed as yet, but as of yesterday I'm the new head of ICU,' he said. 'Brian Yates had to suddenly resign due to ill health.'

She gripped the edges of her coat closer across her chest. *Lucas Banning was her boss?* It put an entirely new spin on things. This first foray of hers into working abroad could be seriously compromised if he decided he didn't want her working with him. And why would he want her here?

She was a living, breathing reminder of the worst mistake he had ever made.

'No,' Molly said. 'I hadn't been informed.'

'Is it going to be a problem?' he asked with a direct look she found a little intimidating.

'Why would it be a problem?' she asked.

'It's a busy and stretched-to-the-limit department,' he said. 'I don't want any personal issues between staff members to compromise patient outcomes.'

Molly felt affronted that he thought her so unprofessional as to bring their past into the workplace. She rarely spoke of Matt these days. Even though she had lived with her grief longer than she had lived without it, speaking of him brought it all back as if it had happened yesterday—the gut-wrenching pain, the aching sense of loss. *The guilt.* Most of her friends from medical school didn't even know she had once had an older brother. 'I do *not* bring personal issues to work,' she said.

His hazel eyes held hers for a beat or two of silence. 'Fine,' he said. 'I'll see you in the morning. Don't be late.'

Molly pursed her lips as he strode off down the street. She would make sure she was there before he was.

Lucas glanced pointedly at the clock on the wall as Molly Drummond rushed into the glassed-in office of ICU. 'Your shift started an hour ago,' he said as he slapped a patient's file on the desk.

'I'm so sorry,' she said breathlessly. 'I tried to call but I didn't have the correct code in my phone. I'm still with my Australian network so I couldn't call direct.'

'So what's your excuse?' he asked, taking in her pink face and the disarray of her light brown hair. 'Boyfriend keep you up late last night, or did he make you late by serving you breakfast in bed?'

Her face went bright red and her grey-blue eyes flashed with annoyance. 'Neither,' she said. 'I was on my way to work when I came across a cat that had been hit by a car. I couldn't just leave it there. It had a broken leg and was in pain. I had to take it to the nearest vet clinic. It took me ages to find one, and then I had to wait until the vet got there.'

Lucas knew he should apologise for jumping to conclusions but he wanted to keep a professional distance. Out of all the hospitals in London, or the whole of England for that matter, why did she have to come to his? He had put as much distance as he could between his past and the present. For the last ten years he had tried to put it behind him, not to forget—he could never, would *never* do that—but to move on with his life as best he could, making a difference where he could.

Saving lives, not destroying them.

Molly Drummond turning up in his world was not what he needed right now. He had only recently found out she was coming to work here, but he had assured himself that he wouldn't have to have too much to do with her directly. He had planned to become director at the end of next year when Brian Yates formally retired. But Brian being diagnosed with a terminal illness had meant he'd had to take over the reins a little ahead of schedule. Now he would have to interact with Molly on a daily basis, which would have been fine if she was just like any other young doctor who came and went in the department.

But Molly was not just any other doctor.

She wasn't that cute little freckle-faced kid any more either. She had grown into a beautiful young woman with the sort of understated looks that took you by surprise in unguarded moments. Like yesterday, when he'd run into her on the street.

Looking up and seeing her there had made his breath catch in his throat. He had been taken aback by the way her grey-blue eyes darkened or softened with her mood. How her creamy skin took on a rosy tinge when she felt cornered or embarrassed. How her high cheekbones gave her a haughty regal air, and yet her perfect nose with its tiny dusting of freckles had an innocent girl-next-door appeal that was totally beguiling. How her figure still had a coltish look about it with those long legs and slim arms.

He had not been able to stop himself imagining how it would feel to have those slim arms wrap around his body and to feel that soft, full mouth press against his. He had his share of sexual encounters, probably not as many as some of his peers, but he wasn't all that comfortable with letting people get too close.

And getting too close to Molly Drummond was something he wanted to avoid at all costs.

'I haven't got time to give you a grand tour,' Lucas said, forcing his wayward thoughts back where they belonged. 'But you'll find your way around soon enough. We have twenty beds, all of them full at the present time. Jacqui Hunter is the ward clerk. She'll fill you in on where the staff facilities are. Su Ling and Aleem Pashar are the registrars. They'll run through the patients with you.' He gave her a brisk nod before he left the office. 'Enjoy your stay.'

'Dr Drummond?'

Molly turned to see a middle-aged woman coming towards her. 'I'm sorry I wasn't here to greet you,' the woman said with a friendly smile. 'Things have been a bit topsy-turvy, I'm afraid.' She offered her hand. 'I'm Jacqui Hunter.'

'Pleased to meet you,' Molly said.

'This has been such a crazy couple of days,' Jacqui said. 'Did Dr Banning tell you about Brian Yates?' She didn't wait for Molly to respond. 'Such a terrible shame. He was planning to retire next year. Now he's been sent home to get his affairs in order.'

'I'm very sorry,' Molly said.

'He and Olivia just had their first grandchild too,' Jacqui said shaking her head. 'Life's not fair, is it?'

'No, it's not.'

Jacqui popped the patient's file, which Lucas had left on the desk, in the appropriate drawer. 'Now, then,' she said, turning to face Molly again. 'Let's get you familiarised with the place. You're from Australia, aren't you? Sydney, right?'

'Yes,' Molly said. 'But I grew up in the bush.'

'Like our Lucas, huh?'

'Yes, we actually grew up in the same country town in New South Wales.'

Jacqui's eyebrows shot up underneath her blunt fringe. 'Really? What a coincidence. So you know each other?'

Molly wondered if she should have mentioned anything about her connection with Lucas. 'Not really. It's been years since I've seen him,' she said. 'He moved to London when I was seventeen. It's not like we've stayed in touch or anything.'

'He's a bit of a dark horse is our Lucas,' Jacqui said, giving Molly a conspiratorial look. 'Keeps himself to himself, if you know what I mean.'

Molly wasn't sure if the ward clerk was expecting a response from her or not. 'Um…yes…'

'No one knows a whisper about his private life,' Jacqui said. 'He keeps work and play very separate.'

'Probably a good idea,' Molly said.

Jacqui grunted as she led the way to the staff change room. 'There's plenty of women around here who would give their eye teeth for a night out with him,' she said.

'It should be a crime to be so good looking, don't you think?'

'Um...'

'He's got kind, intelligent eyes,' Jacqui said. 'The patients love him—and so do the relatives. He takes his time with them. He treats them like he would his own family. That's rare these days, let me tell you. Everyone is so busy climbing up the career ladder. Lucas Banning was born to be a doctor. You can just tell.'

'Actually, I think he always planned on being a wheat and sheep farmer, like his father and grandfather before him,' Molly said.

Jacqui looked at her quizzically. 'Are we talking about the same person?' she asked.

'As I said, I don't know him all that well,' Molly quickly backtracked.

Jacqui indicated the female change room door on her right. 'Bathroom is through there and lockers here,' she said. 'The staff tea room is further down on the left.' She led the way back to the office. 'You're staying three months with us, aren't you?'

'Yes,' Molly said. 'I haven't been overseas before. The job came up and I took it before I could talk myself out of it.'

'Well, you're certainly at the right time of life to do it, aren't you?' Jacqui said. 'Get the travel bug out of the way before you settle down. God knows, you'll never be able to afford it once the kids come along. Take it from me. They bleed you dry.'

'How many children do you have?'

'Four boys,' Jacqui said, and with a little roll of her eyes added, 'Five if you count my husband.' She led the way back to the sterilising bay outside ICU. 'One of the registrars will go through the patients with you. I'd better get back to the desk.'

'Thanks for showing me around.'

Molly spent an hour with the registrars, going through each patient's history. Lucas joined them as they came to the last patient. Claire Mitchell was a young woman of twenty-two with a spinal-cord injury as well as a serious head injury after falling off a horse at an equestrian competition. She had been in an induced coma for the past month. Each time they tried to wean her off the sedatives her brain pressure skyrocketed. The scans showed a resolving intracerebral haematoma and persistent cerebral oedema.

Molly watched as Lucas went through the latest scans with the parents. He explained the images and answered their questions in a calm reassuring manner.

'I keep thinking she's going to die,' the mother said in a choked voice.

'She's come this far,' Lucas said. 'These new scans show positive signs of improvement. It's a bit of a waiting game, I'm afraid. Just keep talking to her.'

'We don't know how to thank you,' the father said. 'When I think of how bad she was just a week ago...'

'She's definitely turned a corner in the last few days,' Lucas said. 'Just try and stay positive. We'll call you as soon as there's any change.'

Molly met his gaze once the parents had returned to their daughter's bedside. 'Can I have a quick word, Dr Banning?' she asked. 'In private?'

His brows came together as if he found the notion

of meeting with her in private an interruption he could well do without. 'My office is last on the left down the corridor. I'll meet you there in ten minutes. I just have to write up some meds for David Hyland in bed four.'

Molly stood outside the office marked with Lucas's name. The door was ajar and she peered around it to see if he was there, but the office was empty so she gently pushed the door open and went inside.

It was furnished like any other underfunded hospital office: a tired-looking desk dominated the small space with a battered chair that had an L-shaped rip in the vinyl on the back. A dented and scratched metal filing cabinet was tucked between the window and a waist-high bookcase that was jammed with publications and textbooks. A humming computer was in the middle of the desk and papers and medical journals were strewn either side. Organised chaos was the term that came to Molly's mind. There was a digital photo frame on the filing cabinet near the tiny window that overlooked the bleak grey world outside. She pressed the button that set the images rolling. The splashes of the vivid outback colour of Bannington homestead took her breath away. The tall, scraggy gum trees, the cerulean blue skies, the endless paddocks, the prolific wildflowers after last season's rain, the colourful bird life on the dams and the waters of Carboola Creek, which ran through the property, took her home in a heartbeat. She could almost hear the *arck arck* sound of the crows and the warbling of the magpies.

Her parents had run the neighbouring property Drummond Downs up until their bitter divorce seven

years ago. It had been in her family for six generations, gearing up for a seventh, but Matthew's death
had changed everything.

Her father had not handled his grief at losing his only
son. Her mother had not handled her husband's anger
and emotional distancing. The homestead had gradually run into the red and then, after a couple of bad sea-
sons, more and more parcels of land had had to be sold
off to keep the bank happy. With less land to recycle
and regenerate crops and stock, the property had been
pushed to the limit. Crippling debts had brought her
parents to the point of bankruptcy.

Offers of help from neighbours, including Lucas's
parents, Bill and Jane Banning, had been rejected. Molly's father had been too proud to accept help, especially
from the parents of the boy who had been responsible
for the death of their only son. Drummond Downs had
been sold to a foreign investor, and her parents had divorced within a year of leaving the homestead.

Molly sighed as she pressed the stop button, her hand
falling back to her side. The sound of a footfall behind
her made her turn around, and her heart gave a jerky
little movement behind her ribcage as she met Lucas's
hazel gaze. 'I was just...' she lifted a hand and then
dropped it '...looking at your photos...'

He closed the door with a soft click but he didn't
move towards the desk. It was hard to read his expression, but it seemed to Molly as if he was controlling
every nuance of his features behind that blank, im-
personal mask. 'Neil emails me photos from time to
time,' he said.

'They're very good,' Molly said. 'Very professional.'

Something moved like a fleeting shadow through his eyes. 'He toyed with the idea of being a professional photographer,' he said. 'But as you know…things didn't work out.'

Molly chewed at the inside of her mouth as she thought about Neil working back at Bannington Homestead when he might have travelled the world, doing what he loved best. So many people had been damaged by the death of her brother. The stone of grief thrown into the pond of life had cast wide circles in the community of Carboola Creek. When Lucas had left Bannington to study medicine, his younger brother Neil had taken over his role on the property alongside their father. Any hopes or aspirations of a different life Neil might have envisaged for himself had had to be put aside. The oldest son and heir had not stepped up to the plate as expected. Various factions of the small-minded community had made it impossible for Lucas to stay and work the land as his father and grandfather had done before him.

'It wasn't your fault,' Molly said, not even realising how firmly she believed it until she had spoken it out loud. She had never blamed him but she had grown up surrounded by people who did. But her training as a doctor had made her realise that sometimes accidents just happened. No one was to blame. If Matt had been driving, as he had only minutes before they'd hit that kangaroo that had jumped out in front of them on the road, it would have been him that had been exiled.

Lucas hooked a brow upwards as he pushed away from the door. 'Wasn't it?'

Molly turned as he strode past her to go behind his

desk. She caught a faint whiff of his aftershave, an intricately layered mix of citrus and spice and something else she couldn't name—perhaps his own male scent. His broad shoulders were so tense she could see the bunching of his muscles beneath his shirt. 'It was an accident, Lucas,' she said. 'You know it was. That's what the coroner's verdict was. Anyway, Matt could easily have been driving instead of you. Would you have wanted him to be blamed for the rest of his life?'

His eyes met hers, his formal back-to-business look locking her out of the world of his pain. 'What did you want to speak to me about?' he asked.

Molly's shoulders went down on an exhaled breath. 'I sort of let slip to Jacqui Hunter that we knew each other from…back home…'

A muscle in his cheek moved in and out. 'I see.'

'I didn't say anything about the accident,' she said. 'I just said we grew up in the same country town.'

His expression was hard as stone, his eyes even harder. 'Why did you come here?' he asked. 'Why this hospital?'

Molly wasn't sure she could really answer that, even to herself. Why had she felt drawn to where he had worked for all these years? Why had she ignored the other longer-term job offers to come to St Patrick's and work alongside him for just three months? It had just seemed the right thing to do. Even her mother had agreed when Molly had told her. Her mother had said it was time they all moved on and put the past—and Matthew—finally to rest. 'I wanted to work overseas but most of the other posts were for a year or longer,' she said. 'I wasn't sure if I wanted to stay away from home quite that long. St Patrick's seemed like a good place to start. It's got a great reputation.'

He barricaded himself behind his desk, his hands on his lean hips in a keep-back-from-me posture. 'I've spent the last decade trying to put what happened behind me,' he said. 'This is my life now. I don't want to destroy what little peace I've been able to scratch together.'

'I'm not here to ruin your peace or your life or career or whatever,' Molly said. 'I just wanted some space from my family. Things have been difficult between my parents, especially since Crystal got pregnant. I'm tired of being the meat in the sandwich. I wanted some time out.'

'So you came right to the lion's den,' he said with an embittered look. 'Aren't your parents worried I might destroy your life too?'

Molly pressed her lips together for a moment. Her father had said those very words in each and every one of their heated exchanges when she'd broached the subject of coming to London. 'Do you want me to resign?' she asked.

His forehead wrinkled in a heavy frown and one of his hands reached up and scored a rough pathway through his hair before dropping back down by his side. 'No,' he said, sighing heavily. 'We're already short-staffed. It might take weeks to find a replacement.'

'I can work different shifts from you if—'

He gave her a dark look. 'That won't be necessary,' he said. 'People will start to ask questions if we make an issue out of it.'

'I'm not here to make trouble for you, Lucas.'

He held her gaze for an infinitesimal moment, but the screen had come back up on his face. 'I'll see you on the ward,' he said, and pulled out his chair and sat down. 'I have to call a patient's family.'

Molly walked to the door, but as she pulled it closed on her exit she saw that he was frowning heavily as he reached for the phone...

CHAPTER TWO

LUCAS WAS GOING through some blood results with Kate Harrison, one of the nurses, when Molly came into the ICU office the following day. Her perfume drifted towards him, wrapping around his senses, reminding him of summer, sweet peas and innocence. How she managed to look so gorgeous this early in the morning in ballet flats and plain black leggings and a long grey cardigan over a white top amazed him. She wasn't wearing any make-up to speak of and her shoulder-length hair was pulled back in a ponytail, giving her a fresh-faced, youthful look that was totally captivating.

'Good morning,' she said, her tentative smile encompassing Kate as well as him.

'Morning,' he said, turning back to the blood results. 'Kate, I want you to keep an eye on Mr Taylor's white-cell count and CRP. Let me know if there's any change.'

'I'll ring you with the results when they come in,' Kate said. She turned to Molly. 'Hi, I'm Kate Harrison. I heard on the grapevine you're from Dr Banning's neck of the woods.'

Molly's gaze flicked uncertainly to Lucas's. 'Um… yes…'

'I looked it up on an internet map,' Kate said. 'It's

a pretty small country town. Were you neighbours or something?'

'Sort of,' Molly said. 'Lucas's family ran the property next door but it was ten kilometres away.'

'I wish my neighbours were ten kilometres away,' Kate said with a grin, 'especially when they play their loud music and party all night. Nice to have you with us, Dr Drummond.'

'Please call me Molly.'

'We have a social club you might be interested in joining,' Kate said. 'A group of us hang out after hours. It's a good way to meet people from other departments. Nobody admits it out loud but it's sort of turned into a hospital dating service. We've had two marriages, one engagement and one and a half babies so far.'

'Dr Drummond already has a boyfriend,' Lucas said as he opened the file drawer.

'Actually, I would be interested,' Molly said, sending him a hard little look. 'Apart from Simon, I don't have any friends over here.'

'Great,' Kate said. 'I'll send you an invite by email. We're meeting for a movie next week.'

Lucas waited until Kate had left before he spoke. 'I'd be careful hanging out with Kate's social group. Not all the men who go have the right motives.'

She gave him a haughty look. 'I can take care of myself.'

'From what I've heard so far about your plastics guy, he doesn't seem your type.'

Her brows came up. 'And you're some sort of authority on who my type is, are you?'

He gave a loose shrug of his shoulders. 'Just an ob-
servation.'

'Then I suggest you keep your observations to yourself,' she said, her eyes flashing like sheet lightning.
'I'm perfectly capable of managing my own private
life. At least I have one.'

'Just because I keep my private life out of the hospital corridors doesn't mean I don't have one,' Lucas
clipped back.

Jacqui came into the office behind them. 'Whoa, is
this pistols at three paces or what?' she said. 'What's
going on?'

'Nothing,' they said in unison.

Jacqui's brows lifted speculatively. 'I thought you
guys were old friends from back home?'

'Excuse me,' Molly said, and brushed past to leave.

'What's going on between you two?' Jacqui asked
Lucas.

'Nothing,' he said with a glower.

'Could've fooled me,' Jacqui said. 'I saw the way she
was glaring at you. It's not like you to be the big bad
boss. What did you say to upset her?'

'Nothing.'

Jacqui folded her arms and gave him a look. 'That's
two nothings from you, which in my book means there's
something. I might be speaking out of turn, but you
don't seem too happy to have her here.'

The last thing Lucas wanted was anyone digging into
his past connection with Molly. It was a part of his life
he wanted to keep separate. The turmoil of emotions
he felt over Matt's death was something he dealt with
in the privacy of his home. He didn't want it at work,

where he needed a clear head. He didn't like his ghosts or his guilt hanging around.

'Dr Drummond is well qualified and will no doubt be a valuable asset to the team at St Patrick's,' he said. 'All new staff members take time to settle in. It's a big change moving from one hospital to another, let alone across the globe.'

'She's very beautiful in a girl-next-door sort of way, isn't she?'

He gave a noncommittal shrug as he leafed through a patient's notes. 'She's OK, I guess.'

Jacqui's mouth tilted in a knowing smile. 'She's the sort of girl most mothers wish their sons would bring home, don't you think?'

Lucas put the file back in the drawer and then pushed it shut. 'Not my mother,' he said, and walked out.

Lucas was walking home from the hospital a couple of days later when he saw Molly coming up the street, carrying a cardboard box with holes punched in it. He had managed to avoid her over the last day or two, other than during ward rounds where he had kept things tightly professional. But as she came closer he could see she looked flustered and upset.

'What's wrong?' he asked as she stopped right in front of him.

Her grey-blue eyes were shiny and moist with tears. 'I don't know what to do,' she said. 'My landlord has flatly refused to allow me to have Mittens in my flat. He's threatening to have me evicted if I don't get rid of him immediately.'

'Mittens?'

She indicated the box she was carrying. 'Mittens the cat,' she said, 'the one that got hit by a car on my first day? I had to take him otherwise the vet would've sent him to the cat shelter and he might've been put down if no one wanted him.'

'Didn't the owner come and claim him?' Lucas asked.

'It turns out he doesn't have an owner, or none we can track down,' she said. 'He hasn't got a collar or a microchip. He's only about seven months old.'

He angled his head, his gaze narrowing slightly. 'What were you planning to do with him?'

Her expression became beseeching. 'One of the nurses mentioned you lived in a big house all by yourself. She said you had a garden that would be perfect for a cat. She said you'd—'

Lucas held up his hands like stop signs. 'Oh, no,' he said. 'No way. I'm not having some flea-bitten cat sharpening its claws on my rugs or furniture.'

'It's only for a few days,' she said, appealing to him with those big wide eyes of hers. 'I'll find another flat, one that will allow me to have a cat. *Please?*'

Lucas could feel his resolve slipping. How was he supposed to resist her when she was so darned cute standing there like a little lost waif? 'I hate cats,' he said. 'They make me sneeze.'

'But this one is a non-allergenic cat,' she said. 'He was probably hideously expensive and now we have him for free. Well…not free exactly…' She momentarily tugged at her lower lip with her teeth. 'The vet's bill was astronomical.'

'I do *not* want a cat,' he said through tight lips.

'You're not getting a cat,' she said. 'You're *babysitting* one.'

Lucas rolled his eyes and took the box from her. His fingers brushed against hers and a lightning strike of electricity shot through his body. Her eyes flared as if she had felt it too, and two little spots of colour pooled high in her cheeks. She stood back from him and tucked a strand of hair back behind her ear, her gaze slipping from his. 'I don't know how to thank you,' she said.

'My place is just along here,' he said gruffly, and led the way.

Molly stepped into the huge foyer of the four-storey mansion Lucas owned. The house was tastefully decorated with an eclectic mix of modern, art deco and antique pieces. Room after room led off the foyer and a grand staircase to the floors above. There was even a ballroom, which overlooked the garden, and a conservatory. It was such a big house for one person. It would have housed three generations of a family with room to spare. 'You don't find it a little cramped?' she asked dryly as she turned and faced him.

The corner of his mouth twitched, which was about the closest he ever got to a smile. 'I like my space,' he said as he shrugged off his coat and hung it on the brass coat rack. 'I guess it comes from growing up in the outback.'

'Tell me about it,' Molly said with feeling. 'I'm starting to feel quite claustrophobic at that bedsit and I've barely been there a week. I don't know why Simon suggested it.'

'Does he live there with you?' he asked.

'No, he's renting a place in Bloomsbury,' she said. 'He offered me a room but I wanted to keep my independence.'

'Are you sleeping with him?'

Molly frowned to cover her embarrassment. She had only slept with Simon once and she had instantly regretted it. She couldn't help feeling he had only slept with her as a sort of payback to his ex Serena because he'd been so hurt by her leaving him. Molly had mistaken his friendliness as attraction, but now she wasn't sure how to get out of the relationship without causing him further hurt. 'I can't see how that is any of your business,' she said.

His eyes remained steady on hers, quietly assessing. 'You don't seem the casual sleep around type.'

She felt her cheeks heat up a little more. 'I'm not a virgin, if that's what you're suggesting. And there's nothing wrong with casual sex as long as it's safe.'

His gaze slowly tracked down to her mouth.

Something shifted in the air—an invisible current that connected her to him in a way Molly had never felt quite before. She felt her lips start to tingle as if he had bent his head and pressed his mouth to hers. She could almost feel the warm, firm dryness of his lips against her own. Her mind ran wild with the thought of his tongue slipping through the shield of her lips to find hers and call it into erotic play. Her insides flickered with hot little tongues of lust, sending arrows of awareness to the very heart of her. She ran the tip of her tongue out over the surface of her lips and watched as his hooded gaze followed its journey.

The mewling cry of Mittens from inside the box broke the spell.

Lucas frowned as if he had completely forgotten what he was carrying. 'Er...aren't we supposed to rub butter on its paws or something?' he asked.

'I think that's just an old wives' tale,' Molly said. 'I'm sure if we show him around first he'll soon work out his territory. I don't suppose you happen to have a pet door?'

He gave her a speaking look. 'No.'

'Oh, well, he'll soon let you know when he wants to go in or out. Maybe you could leave a window open.'

'No.'

Molly pursed her lips in thought. 'How about a kitty litter box? Then you wouldn't have to worry about him getting locked inside while you're at work.'

'Read my lips,' he said, eyeballing her over the top of the box. 'I am *not* keeping this cat. This is an interim thing until you find a pet-friendly place to stay.'

'Fine.' She opened the folded over lid of the box. Mittens immediately popped his head up and mewed at her. 'Isn't he cute?'

'Adorable.'

Molly glanced up at him but he wasn't looking at the cat. 'Um...I brought some food with me,' she said, and rummaged in her handbag for the sample packs the vet had given her.

Mittens wound himself around Lucas's ankles, purring like an engine as his little cast bumped along the floor.

'I think he likes you,' Molly said.

Lucas glowered at her. 'If he puts one paw out of place, it will be off to the cat shelter.'

She scooped the cat up into her arms, stroking his soft, velvety little head as she looked up into Lucas's stern features. 'I'll just feed him and give him his medication and get out of your hair,' she said.

'The kitchen is this way,' he said, and led the way.

Molly stood back to watch as Mittens tucked into the saucer of food she had placed on the floor. 'He's been wormed and vaccinated,' she said.

'Desexed?'

'That too,' she said. 'He might still be a bit tender down there.'

'My heart bleeds.'

Molly picked up her handbag and slung it across her shoulder. 'He'll need to use the bathroom once he's finished eating. Do you know you can actually train a cat to use a human toilet? I saw it on the internet.'

He didn't look in the least impressed. 'How fascinating.'

'Right, well, then,' she said, and made a move for the door. 'I'll leave you to it.'

'What are you doing for dinner?' Lucas suddenly asked.

Molly blinked. 'Pardon?'

His mouth twisted self-deprecatingly. 'Am I that out of practice?'

'What do you mean?'

'I haven't asked anyone to stay to dinner in a while,' he said. 'I like to keep myself to myself once I get home. But since you're here you might as well stay and share a meal with me. That is if you've got nothing better to do.'

'You're not worried what people will think about us socialising out of hours?' she asked.

'Who's going to know?' he said. 'My private life is private.'

Molly felt tempted to stay, more than tempted. She told herself it was to make sure Mittens was settled in, but if she was honest, it had far more to do with her craving a little more of Lucas's company. It wasn't just that he was from back home either. She felt drawn to his aloofness; his don't-come-too-close-I-might-bite aura was strangely attractive. His accidental touch earlier had awoken her senses. She could still feel the tingling of her skin where his fingers had brushed against hers.

'I haven't got anything planned,' she said. 'Simon's going to the theatre with his friend. There wasn't a spare ticket.' She saw his brows lift cynically and hastily added, 'I didn't want to see it anyway.'

Lucas moved across the room to open the French doors that led out to the garden. He turned on the outside light, which cast a glow over the neatly clipped hedges that made up the formal part of the garden. A fountain trickled in the middle of a pebbled area and a wrought-iron French provincial setting was against one wall where a row of espaliered ornamental trees was growing. Mittens bumped his way over and went out to explore his new domain. He stopped to play with a moth that had fluttered around the light Lucas had switched on.

'It's a lovely garden,' Molly said. 'Was it like that when you bought it?'

'It had been a bit neglected,' he said. 'I've done a bit of work on the house too.'

'You always were good with your hands,' she said, and then blushed. 'I mean, with doing things about the farm.'

His lips gave a vague sort of movement that could not on anyone's terms be described as a smile. 'Would you like a glass of wine?' he asked.

'Sure, why not?' Molly said. *Anything to make her relax and stop making a fool of herself,* she thought.

He placed a glass of white wine in front of her. 'I have red if you prefer.'

'No, white is fine,' she said. 'Red always gives me a headache.'

Lucas went about preparing the meal. Molly watched as he deftly chopped vegetables and meat for the stir-fry he was making. He worked as if on autopilot but she could see he was frowning slightly. Was he regretting asking her to stay for dinner? He wasn't exactly full of conversation. But, then, she was feeling a little tongue-tied herself.

'So why an intensivist?' he asked after a long silence. 'I thought you always wanted to be a teacher.'

'My teacher stage only lasted until I was ten,' Molly said. 'I've wanted to be lots of things since then. I decided on medicine in my final year at school. And I chose intensive care because I liked the idea of helping to save lives.'

'Yeah, well, it sure beats the hell out of destroying them.'

Molly met his gaze over the island bench. 'How long are you going to keep punishing yourself? It's not going to bring him back.'

His eyes hardened. 'You think I don't know that?'

Molly watched him slice some celery as if it was a mortal enemy. His jaw was pulsing with tension as he worked. She let out an uneven sigh and put her wine down. 'Maybe it wasn't such a good idea for me to stay and have dinner,' she said as she slid off the stool she had perched on. 'You don't seem in the mood for company. I'll see myself out.'

He caught her at the door. His long, strong fingers met around her wrist, sending sparks of awareness right up to her armpit and beyond. She looked into his eyes and felt her heart slip sideways. Pain was etched in those green and brown depths—pain and something else that made her blood kick-start in her veins like a shot of pure adrenalin. 'Don't go,' he said in a low, gruff tone.

Molly's gaze drifted to his mouth. She felt her insides shift, a little clench of longing that was slowly but surely moving through her body.

His body was closer than it had ever been. She felt the warmth of it, the bone-melting temptation of it. She sensed the stirring of his response to her. She couldn't feel it but she could see it in his eyes as they held hers. It sent an arrow of lust through her. She wanted to feel him against her, to feel his blood surging in response to her closeness. She took a half a step to close the gap between their bodies but he dropped her wrist as if it had suddenly caught fire.

'I'm sorry,' he said, raking that same hand through his thick hair, leaving crooked finger-width pathways in its wake.

'It's fine,' Molly said, aiming for light and airy but falling miserably short. 'No harm done.'

'I don't want you to get the wrong idea, Molly,' he

said, frowning heavily. 'Any...connection between us is inadvisable.'

'Because you don't mix work with play?'

His eyes were hard and intractable as they clashed with hers. 'Because I don't mix emotion with sex.'

'Who said anything about sex?' Molly asked.

His worldly look said it all.

'Right, well...I'm not very good at this, as you can probably tell,' she said, tucking a strand of hair back behind her ear. 'I try to be sophisticated and modern about it all but I guess deep down inside I'm just an old-fashioned girl who wants the fairy-tale.'

'You're no different from most women—and most men, for that matter,' he said. 'It's not wrong to want to be happy.'

'Are *you* happy, Lucas?' Molly asked, searching his tightly set features.

His eyes moved away from hers as he moved back to the kitchen. 'I need to put on the rice,' he said. 'You'd better keep an eye on your cat.'

Molly went outside to find Mittens. He wasn't too happy about being brought back inside, but she lured him back in with a thread she found hanging off her coat. She closed the door once he was inside and went back to where Lucas was washing the rice for the rice cooker. 'What can I do to help?' she said. 'Shall I set the table in the dining room?'

'I don't use the dining room,' he said. 'I usually eat in here.'

'Seems a shame to have such a lovely dining room and never use it,' Molly said. 'Don't you ever have friends over for dinner parties?'

He gave a shrug and pressed the start button on the cooker. 'Not my scene, I'm afraid.'

'Do you have a housekeeper?'

'A woman comes once a week to clean,' he said. 'I don't make much mess, or at least I try not to. I wouldn't have bothered getting anyone but Gina needed the work. Her husband left her to bring up a couple of kids on her own. She's reliable and trustworthy.'

Molly cradled her wine in her hands. 'Do you have a current girlfriend?'

He was silent for a moment. 'I'm between appointments, so to speak.'

She angled her head at him. 'What sort of women do you usually date?'

His eyes collided with hers. 'Why do you ask?'

Molly gave a little shrug. 'Just wondering.'

'I'm not a prize date, by any means,' he said after another long moment. 'I hate socialising. I hate parties. I don't drink more than one glass of alcohol.'

'Not every woman wants to party hard,' she pointed out.

He studied her unwaveringly for a moment. 'Not very many women just want to have sex and leave it at that.'

Molly felt a wave of heat rise up in her body. 'Is that all you want from a partner?' she asked. 'Just sex and nothing else?'

Had she imagined his eyes looking hungrily at her mouth for a microsecond? Desire clenched tight in her core as his gaze tethered hers in a sensually charged lock. 'It's a primal need like food and shelter,' he said. 'It's programmed into our genes.'

Molly was more aware of her primal needs than she

had ever been. Her body was screaming with them, and had been from the moment she had laid eyes on him on the street the other day. It still was a shock to her that she was reacting so intensely to him. She had never thought herself a particularly passionate person. But when she was around him she felt stirrings and longings that were so fervent they felt like they would override any other consideration.

'We're surely far more evolved and civilised than to respond solely to our basest needs?' she said.

His eyes grazed her mouth. 'Some of us, perhaps.'

The atmosphere tightened another notch.

'So how do you get your primal needs met?' Molly asked with a brazen daring she could hardly believe she possessed. 'Do you drag women back here by the hair and have your wicked way with them?'

This time his gaze went to her hair. She felt every strand of it lift away from her scalp like a Mexican wave. Hot tingles of longing raced along her backbone. She felt a stirring in her breasts; a subtle tightening that made her aware of the lace that supported them. Her heart picked up its pace, a tippity-tap-tap beat that reverberated in her feminine core.

His eyes came back to hers, holding them, searing them, penetrating them. 'I'm not going to have my wicked way with you, Molly,' he said.

'But you want to.' *Oh, dear God, had she really just said that?* Molly thought.

'I'd have to be comatose not to want you,' he said. 'But I'm not going to act on it. Not in this lifetime.'

Molly felt an acute sense of disappointment but tried to cover it by playing it light. 'Glad we got that out of the way,' she said, and picked up her wine. 'You're not really my type in any case.'

A short silence passed.

'Aren't you going to ask what my type *is*?' she asked. 'Oh, no, wait. I remember. You already have an opinion on that, don't you?'

'You want someone strong and dependable, loyal and faithful,' he said. 'Someone who'll stick by you no matter what. Someone who'll want kids and has good moral values in order to raise them.'

Molly raised her brows in mock surprise. 'Not such a bad guess. I didn't know you knew me so well.'

'You're like an open book, Molly.'

She dropped her gaze from his. He was seeing far too much as it was. 'I need to use the bathroom,' she said.

'The guest bathroom is just along from the library.'

As Molly came back from the bathroom she took a quick peek at the library. It was a reader's dream of a room with floor-to-ceiling bookshelves stacked with old editions of the classics with a good selection of modern titles. The scent of books and furniture polish gave the room a homely, comfortable feel. She ran her fingers along the leather-bound spines as if reacquainting herself with old friends.

She thought of Lucas in his big private home with only books for company. Did he miss his family? Did he miss the wide, open spaces of the outback? Did he ever long to go home and breathe in the scent of eucalyptus and that wonderful fresh smell of the dusty earth soaking up a shower of rain?

Molly turned from the bookshelves and her gaze

came upon a collection of photographs in traditional frames on the leather-topped antique desk. She picked up the first one—it was one of Lucas with his family at Christmas when he'd been a boy of about fifteen. His parents stood proudly either side of their boys. Lucas stood between his brothers, a hand on each young shoulder as if keeping them in place. All of them were smiling; their tanned young faces were so full of life and promise.

Within two years it would be a very different family that faced the camera. The local press had hounded the Bannings after the accident. And then the coroner's inquiry a few months later had brought the national press to their door. Sensation-hungry journalists had conducted tell-all interviews with the locals. Even though the coroner had finally concluded it had been an accident and Lucas was not in any way to blame for Matt's death, the press had painted a very different picture from the gossip and hearsay they had gleaned locally. They had portrayed Lucas as a wild boy from the bush who had taken his parents' farm vehicle without permission and taken his best friend for a joyride that had ended in his friend's death. Jane and Bill Banning had visibly aged overnight, Lucas even more so. He had gone from a fresh-faced teenager of seventeen to a man twice that age, who looked like the world had just landed on his shoulders.

Molly reached for the other photo on the desk. Her heart gave a tight spasm as she saw Matt's freckled face grinning widely as he sat astride his motocross bike, his blue eyes glinting with his usual mischief.

The last time she had seen her brother he hadn't

been smiling. He had been furious with her for going into his room and finding his stash of contraband cigarettes. She had told their parents and as a result he had been grounded.

For every one of the seventeen years since that terrible day Molly had wished she had never told their parents. If Matt hadn't been grounded he might not have slipped out with Lucas that night behind their parents' backs. Matt had hated being confined. He'd got claustrophobic and antsy when restrictions had been placed on him. It was one of the reasons he had been thrown from the vehicle. He hadn't been wearing a seat belt.

'I thought you might be in here,' Lucas said from the doorway.

Molly put the photo back down on the desk. 'I hadn't seen that picture before,' she said, and picked up another one of Ian and Neil with their current partners. 'Neil's been going out with Hannah Pritchard for quite a while now, hasn't he? Are they planning on getting married?'

'I think it's been discussed once or twice,' he said.

She put the photo down and looked at him. 'Would you go home for the wedding?'

His expression visibly tightened. 'Dinner's ready,' he said. 'We'll have to make it short. I have to go back to the hospital to check on a patient.'

Molly followed him back to the kitchen, where he had set up two places, one at each end of the long table. He seemed distracted as they ate. He barely spoke and he didn't touch his wine. She got the feeling he had only eaten because his body needed food. He seemed relieved when she pushed her plate away and said she was full.

'I'll walk you home on the way,' he said, and reached for his coat.

'You're not going to drive?'

His eyes shifted away from hers as he slipped his hospital lanyard over his neck. 'It's only a few blocks,' he said. 'I like the exercise.'

They walked in silence until they came to the front door of Molly's bedsit. 'I'll let you know as soon as I find another place to rent,' she said. 'I hope it won't be more than a few days.'

'Fine.'

'Thanks for dinner,' she said after a tight little silence. 'I'll have to return the favour some time.'

'You're not obliged to,' he said, and glanced impatiently at his watch. 'I'd better get going.'

'Bye.' Molly lifted her hand in a little wave but he had already turned his back and left.

CHAPTER THREE

LUCAS DIDN'T LEAVE the hospital until close to three a.m. and the streets were deserted as he trudged home. The chilly wind drove ice-pick holes through his chest in spite of his thick woollen coat and scarf. He shoved his hands deep into his pockets and wondered what it was like back home at Carboola Creek. He loathed February in London. It was so bleak and miserable. If the sun did manage to break through the thick wad of clouds it was usually weak and watery, and while the snow was beautiful when it first fell, it all too soon turned to slippery brown slush.

He thought longingly of Bannington Homestead. If he closed his eyes he could almost smell the rain-soaked red dust of the plains. It seemed a lifetime ago since he had felt the bright hot sun on his face.

He opened the door of his house and a piteous meow sounded. 'Damn you, Molly,' he muttered as the little cat came limping towards him with its big possum-like eyes shining in welcome. 'Don't get too comfortable,' he addressed it in a gruff tone. 'You're not staying long.'

The cat meowed again and ribboned itself around his ankles before moving way to play with the fringe of the Persian carpet. Lucas caught a faint whiff of Molly's perfume in the air as he moved through the house. It was strongest in the library, or maybe that was just his imagination. He breathed in deeply. The hint of jasmine and sweet peas teased his nostrils, reminding him of hot summer evenings sitting out on the veranda at the homestead.

He let out a long weary sigh and picked up the photograph of his family. His parents were in their sixties now. They were still working the land alongside Neil. Ian was the other side of town on another property. His parents had come over to London for visits a few times. He had loved having them here but it made it so much harder when they left. His mother always cried. Even his stoic father had a catch in his voice and moisture in his eyes. Lucas had come to dread the airport goodbyes. He hated seeing them so distraught. He had not encouraged them to return and always made some excuse about being too busy to entertain visitors.

Lucas wondered if they missed him even half as much as he missed them. But it was the price he had to pay. He put the photo back down and looked at Matt's photo. He saw echoes of his mate's face in the pretty features of Molly. That dusting of freckles, the same uptilted nose, the same light brown hair with its sun-bleached highlights.

Was that why he felt so drawn to her?

Not entirely.

She was all woman now, a beautiful young woman with the whole world at her feet. He saw the way the male staff and patients looked at her. It was the same way *he* looked at her. He had been so close to pulling her into his arms and kissing her. He had wanted to press his mouth to the soft bow of hers to see if it felt as soft and sweet as it looked.

But he could just imagine how her parents would react if he laid a finger on their precious daughter. He thought of what *his* parents would feel. They wouldn't say anything out loud, but he knew they would find it hard to accept Molly. It wasn't her fault, but any involvement with her would make moving on from the past that much more difficult for them and for him. Did he want her so badly because he knew he couldn't have her? Or was it just that she was everything he had always wanted for himself but didn't feel he deserved?

When Molly got to work the next morning Su Ling, one of the registrars, pulled her over and said in an undertone, 'Keep away from the boss. He's in a foul mood. We had a death overnight—David Hyland in Bed Four. He went into organ failure and Lucas was here until the wee hours with him and the family.'

Molly glanced at the empty bed and felt a sinking feeling assail her. David Hyland had only been forty-two with a wife and two young children. He'd developed complications after routine gall-bladder surgery and Molly had only spoken to his wife the day before about how hopeful they were that he would pull through.

Deaths in ICU were part of the job. Not everyone made it. It was a fact of life. Miracles happened occasionally but there was only so much medicine and critical care could do. She wondered if every death on the unit brought home to Lucas the death that haunted him most.

'Don't you have anything better to do than to stand there staring into space?' Lucas barked from behind her.

Molly swung around to face him. 'I was just—'

'There are two families waiting in the counselling rooms for updates on their loved ones,' he said in a clipped, businesslike tone. 'I would appreciate it if you got your mind on the job.'

'My mind is on the job,' she said. 'I was on my way to speak to the Mitchell family now. Do you have any further updates on Claire that I should make them aware of?'

His eyes looked bloodshot as if he hadn't slept the night before. 'Claire is stable,' he said. 'I can't give them anything other than that. We'll try and wean her off the sedation again tomorrow. We'll repeat the scans then as well.'

Molly watched as he strode away, barking out orders as he went. Megan, one of the nurses, caught her eye and raised her brows meaningfully as she walked past with a catheter bag. 'He obviously didn't get laid last night.'

Molly hoped her face wasn't looking as hot as if felt. 'Obviously not,' she said, and headed off to the counselling room.

Molly was waiting for a coffee at the kiosk later that day when Simon breezed in. 'Hello, gorgeous,' he said, throwing an arm around her shoulders and planting a smacking kiss on her mouth. 'How's tricks?'

Molly tried to wriggle out of his embrace. 'Stop it, Simon. People are watching.'

'Don't be such a cold fish,' he chided as he tried to land another kiss. 'Are you still angry with me for blowing you off last night? I told you the theatre was booked out.'

'I believe Dr Drummond told you to stop.'

Molly felt a shiver run down her spine at that strong, commanding voice. She turned to see Lucas eyeballing Simon the way a Doberman did a small, annoying terrier.

'Who's this?' Simon asked, with a pugnacious curl of his lip.

'This is my boss,' Molly said, blushing in spite of every attempt not to. 'Lucas Banning, head of ICU.'

Simon's lip curled even further. 'Aiming a bit higher, are we?' he said.

Molly wished the floor would open up and swallow her whole. She glanced at Lucas but his expression gave little away apart from a glint of derision in his eyes. She turned back to Simon. 'I'm not sure what you're implying but I would rather you—'

'You won't put out for me but I bet you'll put out for him if he promises to fast-track your career,' Simon said with his sneer still in place.

Molly was desperate to get away before any more people joined the audience. As it was, she could see one of the nurses dilly-dallying over the sweeteners as she shamelessly eavesdropped. 'I think you've got the wrong idea about our friendship, Simon,' she said. 'I'll call you later.'

'You do that,' he said, throwing Lucas a death stare before looking back at her. 'You have some explaining to do.'

Molly walked out of the kiosk without collecting her coffee. She had only gone three or four strides when

Lucas caught up with her. 'Are you out of your mind?' he asked. 'What are you *thinking,* dating that jerk?'

She kept walking with her head held high. 'It's none of your business who I date.'

'I beg to differ,' he said. 'He's distracting you from your work.'

Molly rolled her eyes. 'He's doing no such thing.'

'He's totally wrong for you,' he said. 'I can't believe you can't see it.'

She stopped and glared at him. 'My private life has absolutely nothing to do with you.'

His gaze held hers for a long tense moment and she saw a pulse beating at the edge of his mouth. 'You're right,' he said. 'Go and break your own heart. See if I care.'

Molly frowned as he strode ahead of her down the corridor. She could be mistaken but she could almost swear that was jealousy she had seen glittering in his eyes.

Lucas put some kitten biscuits in the saucer on the floor. Mittens crunched his way through a little pile before lifting his head and giving a soft purring meow of appreciation.

'You're welcome,' Lucas said. 'But don't think for a moment that I'm warming to you because I'm not.'

The doorbell sounded. For a moment he thought he had imagined it. But then it sounded again. He wasn't expecting visitors, he never had them. Even the most fervent religious proselytisers had given up on him.

He opened his front door to find Molly standing there with a shopping bag in one hand. She looked tiny, standing there in the cold. Her coat looked too big for her and her hat and scarf framed her heart-shaped face, giving her an elfin look that was unbelievably cute. 'I've brought more supplies for Mittens,' she said. 'I hope you don't mind me calling in without notice. I was worried you might be running out of food for him.'

'I picked up some more at the corner store on the way home,' he said.

She handed him the bag. 'I won't come in. I'm busy.'

'Going out with lover boy?' Lucas said as he took the bag.

Her eyes clashed with his. 'What's it to you?'

'Nothing,' he said, wishing it was true. 'I just wouldn't like to see you get hurt. He's a player. I heard a rumour he's got his eyes on Prof Hubert's daughter. As career fast tracks go, you can't get much better than that.'

She gave him a cold look and took a step backwards. 'I'd better get going. I'd hate to take advantage of your warm hospitality.'

'Aren't you going to say hello to your cat?' Lucas asked.

She raised her chin. 'I wasn't sure if I was welcome,' she said. 'The way you spoke to me today in ICU was deplorable.'

He leaned a hand on the doorjamb. 'You want me to apologise? Sorry, but I'm not that sort of boss. If you can't suck it up then you'd better find some other job where you can get your ego stroked all day.'

'You were out of line,' she said, shooting him a little glare. 'You know you were. You were taking out your frustration on your staff. That's not how to run a department like ICU.'

'Are you telling me how to do my job?' he asked.

She held his challenging look. 'I'm telling you I won't be bullied and harassed by you just because you had a bad day.'

'Did you happen to speak to David Hyland's wife and family?' Lucas asked. 'They were expecting him to make it. *I* was expecting him to make it. Do you know what it felt like to go out there and tell them he had died while we were trying to resus him?'

'I know what that feels like. I've had to—'

'His wife looked at me as if I had just stabbed her in the heart,' he said. 'The kids looked at me in bewilderment. Those are the faces that keep me awake at night. Not the bureaucrats who insist on reducing admission times whilst contributing nothing to the running of the hospital other than sipping double-shot caramel lattes and shuffling a bit of paperwork around their desks. Not the CEO who hasn't got a clue what it feels like to be up all night, worrying about a desperately ill patient. It's the families that come back to haunt me. They want me—*they expect me*—to make it all better, to fix things. But I can't always do that.'

'I'm sorry,' she said, nibbling at her lip, her eyes losing their defensive glare. 'A death is hard on everyone.'

Lucas blew out a breath and held open the door for her. 'I should warn you that I'm not good company right now.'

'Maybe I'm not looking for good company.'

He closed the door and turned and faced her. 'What are you looking for?'

She gave a little shrug of one of her slim shoulders. 'I'm not sure…just any company, I guess…'

Lucas kept a wide berth even though he wanted to reach for her and hold her close. He wanted to block out the hellish day he'd had with a bit of mindless sex. But sweet little Molly Drummond wasn't the right candidate. He had a feeling it wouldn't be mindless sex with her. Those soft little tender hands of hers would not just unravel him physically. They would reach inside him and unpick the lock on the vault of his soul. 'Would you like a drink or something?' he asked.

'I'm fine,' she said. 'I won't stay long. I just wanted to check on Mittens. Oh, you got him a litter tray.' She turned and smiled up at him disarmingly. It was like a ray of sunshine after a wet week. It seemed to light up the foyer, or maybe that was just his imagination.

'Yeah, well, he kept me awake half the night howling to be let out,' he said, keeping his voice gruff in case she had noticed his guard slipping momentarily. 'I don't mind tossing and turning over patients but I draw the line at stray cats.'

'Do you think he's settling in?'

'I don't think there's any doubt of that,' he said wryly. 'He's taken up residence on the end of my bed. I tried to shoo him off but he was back within minutes.'

She was still smiling at him. 'You big softie,' she said.

Lucas glowered at her. 'Have you found alternative accommodation yet?'

Her smile faded and her shoulders went down in a little slump of defeat. 'I've rung heaps of agencies but there's nothing close to the hospital, or at least none than I can afford. And no one wants to rent a place for just three months. I don't know what else to do. Simon offered to share his place with me but I'm not sure I want to do that.'

Lucas felt as if each and every one of his spare rooms had suddenly developed eyes and was staring at him pointedly. His thoughts zigzagged in his brain. It wasn't as if she would be in the way. He would probably never even run into her. It was a big house. Too big really, but he'd liked the thought of working on something in his spare time. He'd *needed* something to distract himself. He really should have sold it by now and bought some other rundown place to renovate. It seemed a shame that no one but him got to see how comfortable and convenient it was before he moved on. Molly had already hinted at his lack of hospitality. What would it hurt to have a houseguest for a week or two?

'You could always stay here until something becomes available.' He hadn't realised he had said it out loud until he saw the surprised look on her face.

'Here?' she said. 'With you?'

'In one of the spare rooms,' he said. 'I'd charge you rent and expenses. I'm not running a charity.'

'Are you sure?'

Lucas wasn't one bit sure. He still didn't know why he had uttered those words. But he had and he couldn't unsay them. Besides, he was already looking after her wretched cat. Better that she moved in and took charge of its feeding and toileting. It could sleep on her bed, not his. And he would willingly suffer the invasion of his private domain for a week or two rather than see her move in with Simon-up-himself Westbury.

'I'd expect you to do your share of the cooking while you're here,' he said. 'And I would prefer it if you entertained your men friends off site.'

'It's a very generous offer…' Her perfect white teeth nibbled at her lower lip. 'But what if people think we're actually living together as in *living* together…you know, as a couple?'

Lucas couldn't stop a vision of her lying naked in his bed taking over his mind. He wondered what it would be like, waking up beside her each morning. Seeing her sunny smile, feeling her arms around him, smelling the scent of her on his skin, his body sated from long, passionate hours of lovemaking. He pushed the thoughts aside like a row of books toppling off a mantelpiece. 'I don't waste time worrying what other people think,' he said. 'What I do outside the hospital is no one's business but my own.'

'What about our families?' she asked.

He gave her a grim look. 'Don't you mean *your* family?'

'I don't think my mother will have a problem with it,' she said, frowning a little. 'My father is another story.'

'Isn't it time you lived your own life?' he asked. 'You're twenty-seven years old. You shouldn't have to justify your actions to him or anyone.'

'I know,' she said. 'That's one of the reasons I came to London. I wanted to break free. I think my father still sees me as a little girl who needs protecting.'

'Yeah, well, given your choice in men so far, I'm inclined to agree with him,' Lucas said.

'I know Simon gave you the wrong impression,' she

said. 'He's not usually so...possessive. I think it was all show, to tell you the truth.'

'He's a prize jerk,' Lucas said. 'I thought you had much better taste than that.'

Her grey-blue eyes flashed. 'Perhaps I should have you assess every potential partner to see if they meet your exacting standards,' she said. 'Would that satisfy you?'

Lucas had a feeling he wasn't going to be satisfied by anything other than having her to himself, but he wasn't going to admit that to her. She wasn't his to have. He had to remember that. She was his best mate's little sister. Any chance of a future together had died along with Matt. 'Do you need a hand moving your things across?' he asked. 'I have an hour free now.'

His offer to help appeared to mollify her. 'That would be very helpful,' she said. 'Thank you.'

Molly put the last of her things in the spare room furthest away from Lucas's master suite. She still couldn't quite believe he had made her the offer of temporary accommodation, although she suspected it had more to do with discouraging her from moving in with Simon. It was very dog in the manger of him, given he'd made it clear he wasn't going to pursue her himself. Perhaps he wanted to prove to himself that he could keep his hands off her. Lucas's house was certainly big enough for them to avoid intimate contact. They didn't even have to share a bathroom. There were six to choose from as well as his en suite.

But even sharing a space as large as this had its complications. There was her attraction to him, for one thing. She couldn't seem to control it. Every time he looked at her she felt a stirring of longing deep inside. She *ached* to feel his mouth on hers. It was almost an obsession now. She didn't think she would rest until she had tasted him. And then there was his body: that strong, tall body that was so lean and fit and in its prime. She wanted to explore its carved muscles, smooth her hands over the satin-wrapped steel of his back and shoulders, hold him in her hand, feel the throb of his blood against her palm. Her body got moist thinking about it. Her nerves got twitchy and restless, the contraction-like pulse deep and relentless in her core.

She gave herself a mental shake. She was probably only fixated on him because he had said he wasn't interested in acting on his attraction to her. It was the contrariness of human nature—wanting something you knew you couldn't have.

Molly took Mittens with her downstairs and placed him on the floor near his kitten milk and biscuits. It was raining outside; the droplets of water were rolling like diamonds down the glass of the windows and French doors. It was hard not to think of home when the weather was so dismal. The cold seemed to seep right into her bones. The bedsit had felt like an icebox, but at least Lucas's house was warm, even if his manner towards her was not.

She heard his firm tread behind her as he came into the room. 'Are you all settled in?' he asked.

'Yes, thank you,' Molly said, turning to face him. 'It's a lovely room and so spacious. Much nicer than the bedsit, I can assure you.'

He gave her one of his brisk, businesslike nods. 'I'm

going out for a while,' he said. 'I have some paperwork to see to at the hospital.'

'You work too hard,' she said.

'I get paid to work hard.'

'Surely not this hard,' Molly said. 'You look like you didn't sleep at all last night. Why do you drive yourself so relentlessly? No, don't tell me. I already know.'

His mouth flattened grimly. 'I would prefer it if you kept your opinions to yourself. You might currently share my house but that's all you're going to share. I don't need you to take on the role of a caring partner. Do I make myself clear?'

'When was the last time you had a partner?' Molly asked.

It was a moment or two before he spoke. She wondered if he was trying to remember. 'I can assure you I'm no monk,' he said.

'Tell me the last time you had sex.'

His brows snapped together. 'What *is* this? Do you really think I'm going to give you a blow-by-blow account of my sex life?'

'You've felt at perfect liberty to comment on mine,' Molly pointed out.

'That's because you were conducting it in the hospital cafeteria.'

'That is not true!' she said.

'You'd better keep a lid on your public displays of affection if you want to keep your job,' he said.

Molly felt her back come up. 'Are you threatening me?'

His eyes warred with hers. 'Not personally, but I think I should inform you the current CEO is a stickler

for professional behaviour at all times,' he said. 'Patients
come to St Patrick's for health care, not to witness a
cheesy soap-opera love scene in the middle of the corridor. If a patient complains to him it would be one look
at the CCTV and you'd be fired on the spot.'

'And I bet you'd be the first to be glad to see me go,'
she said with a resentful look.

'So far I've heard nothing but good reports about you
from patients and staff alike,' he said. 'I would hate to
see all that come undone by behaviour that would be
considered puerile in a high school, let alone in a professional setting.'

Molly set her mouth tightly. 'I can assure you it won't
happen again.'

'Make sure that it doesn't,' he said, and strode out.

When Molly came downstairs in the morning Lucas
had already left for work. His housekeeper was in the
kitchen, unloading the dishwasher. She smiled and
straightened as Molly came in. 'I'm Gina,' she said.
'Dr Banning told me you and the little cat are staying
for a few days.'

'Yes,' Molly said. 'I hope that's not going to make
extra work for you?'

'Not at all,' Gina said. 'It will be good for Dr Banning to have some company in this big old house of his.
You're from his home town in Australia, yes?'

'Is my accent that obvious?' Molly asked with a self-
deprecating smile.

'Not your accent,' Gina said. 'Your looks.'

'My...looks?'

'The photo in the library,' Gina said. 'You're Matthew Drummond's sister, yes?'

Molly frowned. 'You know about Matt?'

Gina nodded solemnly. 'Dr Banning's mother told me when they visited a few years ago. Very sad. Such a tragic accident.'

'Yes…yes, it was.'

'It is good that you are still friends,' Gina said.

Friends? Molly thought. Is that what she and Lucas were? 'Um…yes,' she said. 'Our parents were neighbours for years and years. We sort of all grew up together, same school, same teachers even.'

'He is a very kind man,' Gina said. 'But he works too hard. I tell him he needs to find a nice girl, get married and have some kids. It would help him to have something other than work to occupy his mind, yes?'

'Um…he does seem very career driven,' Molly said.

'He uses work to forget,' Gina said. 'He saves lots of lives but he can never bring back the one he wanted to save the most.' She shook her head. 'Sad, very sad.'

Molly gave the housekeeper a pained smile. 'I have to get going,' she said. 'It was lovely meeting you.'

'I hope you're still here when I come next week, yes?' Gina said with a twinkle in her chocolate-brown eyes.

'Oh, no,' Molly said hurriedly. 'I hope to find another flat well before then.'

'Have you found another flat?' Jacqui asked in the staff tearoom a couple of days later.

Molly closed the newspaper rental guide with a dispirited sigh. 'I've looked at five so far but none of them allow pets,' she said. 'The ones I've looked at that do allow them are not fit for an animal, let alone a human. I swear the last one I looked at, even the vermin have packed up and left in disgust.'

'So how's it working out at Lucas's place?' Jacqui asked.

Molly trained her gaze on her mug of tea rather than meet the ward clerk's eyes. She had hoped to keep her temporary living arrangements a secret but apparently someone from the hospital had seen her walking out of Lucas's front door a couple of mornings ago. It had been all over the hospital by the time she'd got to work. If Lucas was bothered about his private life being a topic of public speculation, he hadn't mentioned it, but, then, she hadn't seen him other than in passing, and bringing up the topic at work, even in the privacy of his office, wasn't something she was keen to do. She suspected he was avoiding her but, then, she could hardly talk. She had kept well out of his way too.

'It's fine,' she said. 'I don't see much of him. I see more of him here, to be honest.'

'You could've knocked me down with a feather when I heard you were shacking up with him,' Jacqui said. 'As far as I know, no one from here has even stepped inside his place.'

'I'm not "shacking up" with him,' Molly said, trying not to blush. 'He very kindly offered me a room for a few days.'

'Has he made a move on you?'

Molly pushed her chair back and took her teacup to the sink. 'We don't have that sort of relationship,' she said. 'We're just...housemates.'

Jacqui angled her head at her speculatively. 'You'd

make a nice couple, you know. It's kind of sweet you grew up in the bush together. Kind of a friends-to-lovers thing.'

'I'm a bit over men at the moment,' Molly said. She'd been keeping her distance from Simon over the last couple of days. After his altercation with Lucas in the cafeteria he had increased his pressure on her to move in with him, but she didn't like being used as a pawn in a game of one-upmanship.

'I thought you were seeing someone—Simon what's his name? The plastics registrar.'

'Simon Westbury,' Molly said. 'Yes, well, I've been trying to get out of that relationship for a while now. I shouldn't have got into it in the first place.'

Jacqui tapped her lips thoughtfully. 'Mmm, I can definitely see it.'

'See what?'

'You and Lucas,' Jacqui said. 'I think you two would be a perfect match.'

'Not going to happen,' Molly said flatly. 'Dr Banning is not interested in me. Quite frankly, he can't wait to see the back of me. He hates it that I came here. He thinks I only came to cause trouble for him.'

'Yes, I've been picking up on that vibe,' Jacqui said. 'But why would he think that?'

Molly blew out a breath and pushed open the door to leave. 'Never mind,' she said. 'I have to get back. I'll see you down there.'

CHAPTER FOUR

Lucas was in his office, writing up some notes, when he got a call from Alistair Brentwood in Accident and Emergency. He'd had hundreds of calls over the years from various doctors in A and E, but something about this one made the hairs on the back of his neck stand up as soon as Alistair gave him the rundown on the incoming patient.

It was like hearing his and Matt's accident replayed back to him. The names and ages had changed but it was so similar he felt like he had been swept up in a time warp. The horror of that night came back to him in hammer blows of dread. He felt them pound through his blood as he listened to his colleague's description.

'Lucas, we've got a male, twenty-one, with a serious head injury,' Alistair said. 'Blunt chest trauma and haemodynamically stable. I can see a bit of lung contusion on his chest CT, abdo is OK, but his brain scan looks like global contusions and oedema. His GCS was three at the scene but picked up to six in here. One pupil fixed and dilated, the other sluggish. Pretty serious closed head injury. You got a bed for him up there?'

'Thanks,' Lucas said, mentally gearing up to face the shattered family. He would have to deal with them on a daily basis, helping them come to terms with the severity of their loved one's injuries. 'We're right to take him. Have the neurosurgeons assessed him yet?'

'Yes, they'll put in an ICP monitor when he's settled in the unit. If he survives it's going to be a long haul,' Alistair said matter-of-factly. 'Name's Tim Merrick, he was the passenger. The driver got off very lightly—a Hamish Fisher. He's going to the ward for obs.'

Lucas felt a cold hand press hard against his sternum. *Two shattered families*, he thought. Lives that just hours ago had been normal would now never be normal again. He wondered if Hamish Fisher had any idea of what lay ahead for him—the guilt, the despair, and the what-ifs and if-onlys that would haunt his days and nights for the rest of his life. 'OK. I'll come down now if he's ready,' he said.

'Yeah, he's fine to go.'

'Dr Drummond, this is Tim Merrick, twenty-one-year-old male from a MVA,' Lucas said with his usual clinical calm as the patient was transferred to ICU. *Just another patient*, he kept saying inside his head, but it wasn't working as it normally did. This was somebody's son, someone's brother.

Someone's best friend.

A cold, sick feeling curdled his stomach. Bile rose in his throat. His chest felt as if it was being compressed by an industrial vice. He was having trouble breathing. He could feel sweat beading between his shoulder blades. His temples pounded.

Scenes from seventeen years ago kept flashing through his mind on rapid replay. Matt's parents looking ashen and gutted as they came in to where their son's broken and bloodied body lay on a hospital gurney. Molly standing there, holding her mother's hand, her grey-blue eyes wide with fear and dread, her little face as white as milk but for the nutmeg-like dusting of her freckles. Lucas's parents looking shocked. Their faces seeming to age in front of him as he falteringly tried to explain what had happened.

The doctors with their calm clinical voices and the police with their detached demeanours as they took down his statement and asked questions he could barely answer for the ropey knot of anguish that had risen in his throat.

Lucas blinked a couple of times and brought himself back to the moment. 'He's got a severe closed head injury, but not much else. Neurosurgery are coming up in twenty minutes to put in an ICP monitor. Can you set him up on the ventilator?'

'Sure,' Molly said.

'I'm going to start mannitol and steroids, and do the paperwork,' he said. 'Some relatives have just arrived. I'll go and talk with them. We're going to pull out every stop here to give him a chance of recovery.'

'I'll run the CO2 slightly up and put in a central line, and get the ICP monitor set up ready to connect,' Molly said.

'Good,' Lucas said. 'He's got right pulmonary contusion, and I've just got the official CT report. He's also got a small pneumothorax on the right.'

'Good that was picked up,' Molly said. 'We could've blown that up overnight on the ventilator. I'll put in a right chest drain after I've set the ventilator.'

'Thanks.' He drew in a heavy breath that felt like it had a handful of thumbtacks attached. 'I'll talk to the relatives. He's got a severe head injury, but he could recover. He's only young. He's got to be given the maximum chance.'

Once Molly had put in Tim Merrick's chest drain she went back to the central office where Aleem Pashar was going through the patient notes that had come up from A and E.

'Not sure why the boss is insisting pulling out all the stops,' Aleem said. 'The CT scan's not looking good. Look.'

Molly took the report and read through it with a sinking heart. A positive outcome was very unlikely. What had Lucas been thinking? Surely he of all people knew the data on severe brain injuries? It wasn't fair to give the family unrealistic expectations. They needed to be gently prepared for the imminent loss of their loved one. It might be days, or weeks, sometimes even months, but someone as badly injured as Tim Merrick might not leave ICU alive, or if he did, he would be severely compromised.

'I sure wouldn't want to be the one who was driving,' Aleem said as he leaned back against the desk. 'Can you imagine living with that for the rest of your life?'

Molly frowned as she looked at the registrar. 'Pardon?'

'Tim Merrick's mate,' he said. 'He was the one driving. All he got was a fractured patella.'

Molly bit her lip. Was that why Lucas was doing everything he could to keep Tim alive? He was reliving his own nightmare through the driver. He would be feeling the anguish of the young man, having been through it himself. Keeping Tim Merrick on life support indefinitely was his way of giving the young driver time to come to terms with what had happened. But while she understood Lucas's motives, she wasn't sure she agreed with giving the family false hope. They could end up suffering more in the long run.

'No alcohol involved, which is one thing to be grateful for, I suppose,' Aleem said. 'Apparently he swerved to avoid a kid on a bike. Missed the kid but as good as wrote off his best mate. Can you imagine having that on your conscience? I'd never get behind the wheel again.'

Molly put down the CT report. 'I think I'll have a word with Tim's parents. Dr Banning should be finished with them now.' She turned at the door. 'Can you ring the orthopaedic ward and find out the driver's name? I think I'll visit him before I go home.'

'Will do,' Aleem said, and reached for the phone.

'Mr and Mrs Merrick?' Molly gently addressed the middle-aged couple who were still sitting huddled together in the counselling room.

There was no sign of Lucas, although Molly could pick up a faint trace of his light aftershave in the small room, suggesting he had not long ago left. A pile of used tissues was on the table beside the wife and she had another one screwed up in her hand. The husband was dry-eyed but his Adam's apple was going up and down like a piston.

'I'm Dr Drummond,' Molly said. 'I've been looking after your son in ICU. He's on the ventilator now and comfortable.'

'Can we see him?' the wife asked, absently tearing the tissue in her hand into shreds.

'Yes, of course,' Molly said. 'But first…I think I should warn you that ICU can be an upsetting place. There are lots of machines making all sorts of noises. You are free to come and go as you like but we have a strict hygiene policy to reduce the risk of infection. Did Dr Banning go through all this with you?'

The wife nodded. 'He said Tim's stable for the time being. He said we should talk to him as much as possible…that it might help bring him round.'

'It will certainly do no harm to sit with him and talk to him,' Molly said. 'Has Dr Banning been through Tim's scans with you?'

'He said it's too early to be certain what's going on,' the husband said. 'There's a lot of swelling and bleeding. He said he'd like to wait till that settles before giving a more definitive diagnosis.'

Molly could see the sense in what Lucas had told the Merricks but she wondered if he was just buying time. She had seen the scans. Bleeding and swelling notwithstanding, Tim was critically injured and nothing short of a miracle could turn things around.

She took the parents to their son's bedside and watched as they spoke to him and touched him. It was heart-wrenching to think that in a few days they might lose him for ever.

It was impossible not to think about her brother's death at times like this, how that night in A and E had been such a surreal nightmare. Her parents had done the same as the Merricks. They had touched and stroked Matt, talking to him even though they had already been told he had gone. Molly had seen Lucas on their way out of the hospital. He had been standing with his parents, his face so stricken it had been like looking at someone else entirely. Matt had lost his life, but in a way so too had Lucas. Nothing would ever be the same for him again.

'Dr Drummond?' Mrs Merrick's voice interrupted Molly's reverie. 'Can I talk to you for a minute?'

'Sure,' Molly said.

Mrs Merrick looked at her son again, tears rolling down her face. She brushed at them with her hand and turned back to Molly. 'Tim would hate to be left an invalid. He wouldn't cope with it. We talked about it only recently. A relative—his cousin—had a serious accident at work and was left a quadriplegic. He's totally dependent on carers for everything now.

'Tim said it would destroy him to be left like that. That he would rather die. He insisted on drawing up an end-of-life directive. We tried to talk him out of it. We thought only old or terminally ill people signed them but he was adamant. I suppose what I'm saying is…I want to know what we're dealing with here. I want to do the right thing by my son. I want to be…' She glanced at her husband and continued, '*We* want to be prepared for whatever is ahead.'

'I understand,' Molly said. 'We'll keep you well informed on Tim's progress. There are protocols to go through in regard to end-of-life directives. I'll speak to Dr Banning about it.'

'There's one other thing,' Mr Merrick said as he

came and stood by his wife. 'I want to be clear on this. We don't blame Hamish for what happened to Tim. This is an accident—a terrible, tragic accident. It could've been the other way round. We're devastated for Hamish as well as ourselves.'

Molly felt a lump come up in her throat. She could remember all too well the dreadful words her father had shouted at Lucas and his parents in A and E all those years ago. Everyone had known it had been the raw grief talking but it hadn't made it any easier to witness. If only her father had demonstrated even a fraction of the dignity and grace of the Merricks. 'I'm going to see Hamish now,' she said. 'I'll tell him you're thinking of him.'

Molly went to the orthopaedic ward where Hamish Fisher was spending the night prior to having his knee repaired the following morning. She found him lying in a four-bed ward with the curtains drawn around his bed. Curled up there with his back to the room, he looked a lot younger than twenty-one. Her heart ached for him. He looked so alone and broken. From this day forward his life would never be the same. She wondered if in seventeen years' time he would be just as locked away and lonely as Lucas.

'Hamish?' she said. 'I'm one of the ICU doctors, Molly Drummond.'

Hamish opened his reddened eyes. 'He's dead, isn't he?' he said in a bleak tone.

'No,' she said, taking the chair beside the bed. 'He's on a ventilator and at this point he's stable.'

The young man's chin shook as he fought to control

his emotion. 'But he's going to die, isn't he?' he said. 'I heard the ER doctors talking.'

'No one can say for sure at this stage,' Molly said.

He swallowed convulsively. 'I swerved to avoid a kid on a bike,' he said. 'It all happened so quickly. I saw this little kid coming out of nowhere and I hit the brakes but there must have been oil on the road. I lost control...'

Molly put her hand on his where it was gripping the sheet with white-knuckled force. 'Tim's parents don't blame you,' she said. 'They're with Tim now but I'm sure they'll come down to see you when they get the chance. Do you have anyone here with you? Your parents?'

He shook his head. 'I haven't got a dad. My mum is on her way. She's been on a cruise with friends. She'd saved up for years to go... She's flying home tonight.'

'It's important you have people around to support you,' Molly said. 'I can organise for the hospital chaplain to visit you. It helps to talk to someone at a time like this.'

'Talking isn't going to turn back the clock, is it?' Hamish said.

She gave his hand another squeeze. 'Just try and take it one day at a time.'

Molly didn't see Lucas again until later that night. He came in just before midnight, his face looking drawn and his eyes hollow, as if two fingers had pushed them right back into his head.

'Are you OK?' she asked, rising from the sofa where she had been flicking through a home renovating magazine without managing to remember a word of what she had read.

He scraped a hand through his hair. 'Yeah,' he said. 'Why wouldn't I be? It was just another day at the office.'

'It was hardly that,' Molly said.

He dismissed her with a look and turned to leave. 'I'm going to bed.'

'Lucas?'

His back looked concrete tight with tension in that infinitesimal moment before he turned to look at her. 'I've handled hundreds of critically ill trauma patients,' he said. 'This is just another case.'

She came over to where he was standing. 'It's not just another case,' she said. 'It's like you and Matt all over again.'

A stone mask covered his features. 'Leave it, Molly.'

'I think we should talk about it,' she said. 'I think my parents should've talked to you about it long ago. It was wrong to blame you the way they did. Tim's parents are obviously shattered by what's happened but at least they're not blaming Hamish.'

'That will come later,' he said grimly.

'I don't think so,' she said. 'I think they realise it could just have easily been Tim behind that wheel. It's devastating for them to face the prospect of losing their son but—'

'They are *not* going to lose their son,' Lucas said with implacable force.

Molly frowned at him. 'Lucas, you can't possibly think he's going to survive more than a few days or a week or two at the most.'

A thread of steel stitched his mouth into a flat, determined line. 'I've seen plenty of critically injured patients come off ventilators. He deserves every chance to make it. I'm not withdrawing support.'

'But what if that's not what Tim would've wanted?'

'We'll find out what he wants when he wakes up,' he said.

'What if he doesn't wake up?' Molly asked. 'You saw the scans. It's not looking good right now.'

'Early scans can be misleading,' he said. 'You know that. There's bleeding and swelling everywhere. It can take days or even weeks to get a clear idea of what's going on.'

'I don't think it's fair to give his family false hope,' she said. 'I think they're the sort of people who need to know what they're up against right from the get-go. They want to be prepared.'

His eyes were hard as they clashed with hers. 'I hate to pull rank here but I have a lot more clinical experience than you,' he said. 'His parents are still in shock. This is not the time to be dumping unnecessary and distressing information on them.'

'Tim Merrick signed an end-of-life directive,' Molly said. 'His mother told me. They all did it a couple of years ago after a relative was made a quadriplegic in a workplace accident.'

Lucas drew in a short breath and then slowly released it. 'So?'

'So his wishes should be acknowledged,' Molly said. 'He didn't want to be left languishing in some care facility for the rest of his life. Evidently he was quite adamant about it. He couldn't bear the thought of being dependent on others for everything.'

He moved to the other side of the room, his gait stiff and jerky as if his inner turmoil was manifested in his body. He rubbed the back of his neck. The sound of his hand moving over his skin was amplified in the silence.

'He would want the ventilator turned off, Lucas.'

'It's too early to decide that.'

'There might be a time when it's too late to decide,' Molly pointed out. 'What will you say to him then? "Sorry, we disregarded your directive because we thought you were going to wake up and be back to normal"?'

He cut his gaze to hers. 'I've seen patients with much worse injuries walk out of ICU,' he said.

Molly gave him an incredulous look. 'You think Tim Merrick is going to walk when he can't even *breathe* on his own? Come on, Lucas, surely you haven't abandoned the science you were trained to respect and rely on? He's not going to walk again. He's probably not going to do anything for himself again. And you're prolonging his and his family's agony by insisting on keeping him hooked up to that ventilator.'

'What about Hamish Fisher?' he asked, nailing her with a look.

Molly released a little breath. 'Lucas, it's not Hamish Fisher lying in that bed.'

'No,' he said. 'But he's the one who's going to spend the rest of his life wishing to hell it had been.'

Molly felt the anguish behind his statement. She saw the agony of it on his face. For all these years he would have given anything to trade places with her brother.

But that's not how fate had decided things would be. 'I know this is difficult for you,' she said. 'But you have to keep your clinical hat on. You can't let what happened to you all those years ago influence your decision in managing Tim Merrick's care.'

He looked at her for a long, tense moment. 'Just give him some time,' he said. 'Surely he deserves that?'

'Are we talking about Tim or Hamish?' Molly asked.

He walked to the other side of the room and looked out of the window at the blizzard-like conditions outside. Molly saw his shoulders rise and fall as he let out a long, jagged sigh. She wanted to go to him, to wrap her arms around him and hold him close. But just as she took the first step towards him he turned and looked at her.

'I had a patient a few months back,' he said, 'a young girl of nineteen who'd fallen from a balcony at a party. She fell five metres onto concrete. It was a miracle she survived the fall. She had multiple fractures, including a base-of-skull fracture. She was in a coma for a month. Just when she was showing signs of waking up she got meningitis. The scans looked as if things were going downhill. Every other doctor and specialist involved with her care was ready to give up. I refused to do so. In my view, she just needed more time. I was right. She was young and fit and her other injuries were healing well. After another week she started to improve. It was slow but sure. She's back at university now, doing a fine arts degree. She comes in now and again and brings cupcakes for us all.'

'I'm glad it worked out that way for you and for her,'

Molly said. 'But there are just as many cases where it doesn't.'

He held her look for a long moment. 'The day she walked out of hospital with her parents I went to my office and closed the door and cried like a baby.'

Molly could picture him doing it. He had depths to his character that could so easily go unnoticed in a brief encounter. He was dedicated and professional at all times and yet he was as human as the next person. It was perhaps his humanity that made him such a wonderful ICU doctor. He didn't want anyone to suffer as he had suffered. He worked tirelessly to give his patients the best possible chance of recovery.

His own personal tragedy had moulded him into the man he was today—strong, driven and determined. He was a leader, not a follower. He expected a lot from his staff but he didn't ask anything of them he wasn't prepared to do himself. She could not think of a more wonderful ally in the fight for a patient's life. But she wondered if it all took its toll on him personally. Was that why he was all work and no play? He simply had nothing left to given anyone outside work.

'It must have been an amazing moment to see her walk out of hospital,' she said.

'It was,' he said. 'I know doctors are meant to keep a clinical distance. You can't make sound judgements when your emotions are involved. But once the patient is in the clear, sometimes the relief is overwhelming. I've had staff go on stress leave after a patient leaves. It's those sorts of miracles that make our jobs so rewarding and yet so utterly demanding.'

'How do you deal with the stress?' she asked.

'I fix stuff.'

'Fix stuff?'

He wafted a hand at their surroundings. 'There's nothing quite like tearing down a wall or painting or replastering or refitting a kitchen or bathroom,' he said. 'I'm thinking of selling in the spring. I've just about run out of things to do.'

'But this is such a fabulous house,' Molly said.

He gave a shrug. 'It's just a roof and four walls.'

'It's much more than that, surely?' she said. 'You've put so much work into it. It seems a shame not to get the benefit of it for a while.'

'Don't worry,' he said as he hooked his jacket over one shoulder. 'I'll give you plenty of notice before I let the realtor bring potential buyers through.'

Molly bit her lip. 'I'm having trouble finding anywhere else to live so far.'

'There's no hurry. You can stay here as long as you need to.'

'But not for the whole three months.'

He held her look for a beat. 'I can't imagine that you'd want to. I'm not the most genial host.'

'I think it's best if I keep looking,' she said. 'I'm having a hard time convincing everyone we're not a couple.'

'And that embarrasses you?'

Molly found his green and brown gaze mesmerising. 'No, not at all,' she said. 'Does it embarrass you?'

His eyes moved over her face, as if he was committing her features to memory. The silence throbbed with a backbeat of electric tension. She felt it echoing in her blood and wondered if he could feel it too. His eyes dropped to her mouth, pausing there for an infinitesimal moment. 'In another life I would've kissed you the other night,' he said in a gravel-rough tone. 'I probably would've taken you to bed as well.'

Molly looked at his mouth. She could see the tiny vertical lines of his lower lip and the slight dryness that she knew would cling to her softer one like sandpaper does to silk. 'Why not in this life?' she asked softly.

He reached out and brushed her lower lip with the pad of his index finger. His touch was as light as a moth's wing but it set off a thousand bubbly, tingly sensations beneath her skin. 'I think you know why not,' he said, and stepped back from her.

Molly felt like the floor of her stomach had dropped right out of her as he turned and left the room. She put her hand to her mouth, touching where his finger had so briefly been…

CHAPTER FIVE

LUCAS LOOKED AT the bedside clock and groaned. Another hour had gone by and he still couldn't sleep. His body felt restless, too wired to relax enough to drift off. He wondered if Molly was faring any better. But of course that was his problem—thinking about Molly.

He couldn't *stop* thinking about her. About how soft her plump lower lip had felt against the soft press of his fingertip. How luminous her grey-blue eyes had been when she had looked at him. How husky and sexy her voice had sounded. How he had wanted to pull her into his arms and kiss her, to taste her, to feel her respond to him.

He groaned again and threw off the bedcovers. Having her under the same roof was a form of self-torture. What had he been thinking, inviting her to stay with him? The house had changed since she'd moved in. And it wasn't just her little cat, who right at this moment was curled up on the foot of his bed, purring like an engine.

Molly made his big empty house seem warm and inviting. It was subtle things, like the way she had brought a bunch of flowers home and put them on the kitchen table in a jam jar because he hadn't ever thought to buy a vase. It was the fragrance of her perfume that lingered in the rooms she had wandered into. It was seeing the little array of girly things in the guest bathroom she was using—the lotions and potions, the hairdryer and straightening iron. And it was the not-so-subtle things, like her sexy black wisp of lace knickers hanging to dry over the clotheshorse in the laundry.

It wasn't just the house that had changed since she'd moved in. *He* had changed. He no longer came home wanting to be alone. He came home and looked forward to seeing her, hearing her, being with her. It wasn't enough to see her at work. He wanted more. He wanted to talk to her and to have her talk to him. He wanted to see her smile, hear her laugh.

He wanted her.

But he couldn't have her without the past overshadowing everything. How long before her parents—either singularly or jointly—expressed their misgivings? Such antagonism would poison any alliance between them as a couple. But it wasn't just the family stuff that gave him pause. How could he make her happy when he had nothing to offer her? He was used to being alone. He didn't know how to live any other way. He would end up hurting her, just like he hurt everyone who dared to care about him.

Molly was out of his league, out of bounds, forbidden.

But he still wanted her.

Molly woke to the sound of mewing outside her door. She threw off the bedcovers and padded over to let Mittens in. 'So now you want to sleep in my room, do you, you traitorous feline?' she said.

The little cat blinked up at her guilelessly and mewed again.

'Don't just sit there looking at me like that,' Molly said. 'Are you coming in or not?'

Mittens wound his body around her ankles and then padded off towards the stairs, stopping every now and again to look back at her as if to tell her to follow him.

Molly shook her head in defeat and reached for a wrap. She followed the cat to the kitchen downstairs, where she poured some cat biscuits into the dish on the floor and watched as he munched and crunched his way through them. 'You'd better not make a habit of this,' she muttered. 'I can't see Lucas waiting on you whisker and paw for nocturnal top-ups.'

There was a sound behind her and Molly turned and saw Lucas standing there dressed in nothing but a pair of long black silk pyjama trousers that were loose around his lean hips. Her eyes drank in the sight of his broad muscular chest. The satin skin with its natural tan, the carved pectoral muscles, the tiny pebbles of his flat male nipples, the ripped line of his abdomen and the dark hair that trailed beyond the waistband of the trousers. 'Um…I was just feeding Mittens,' she said, waving a hand at the cat, who was now licking his paws and wiping them over his face in a grooming session.

'So I see,' Lucas said.

'I hope I didn't wake you, nattering away to him,' Molly said.

'I wasn't asleep.'

She looked at his drawn features—the bloodshot eyes, the deep grooves that ran each side of his mouth. *Don't stare at his mouth!* She brought her gaze back up to his eyes and felt a tremor of want roll through her. He was so arrantly sexy with his dark stubbly regrowth and his hair all tousled.

'Can I make you a hot drink or something?' she asked, and started bustling about the kitchen to stop herself from reaching for him. 'I bought some chocolate buttons the other day. They're my weakness. That's why I put them on the top shelf, so they're not in my face and tempting me all the time.' She reached up on tiptoe in the pantry but she couldn't quite reach the packet in her bare feet.

Lucas's arm reached past her and took the packet of chocolate buttons off the shelf. 'Here you go,' he said.

He was *incredibly* close in the tight space. Molly could smell his warm male smell. She could see the individual points of his raspy regrowth along his jaw. She could see the dark flare of his pupils as he held her gaze in a lock that had distinctly erotic undertones. Her fingers touched his as she went to take the packet from him but he didn't release it. She gave it a little tug but still he held firm. She nervously sent the tip of her tongue out over her lips and gave the packet another little tug.

She felt the faintest loosening of his hold, but just as she was about to claim victory, his fingers wrapped around hers. The electricity of his touch sent a shockwave through her senses.

He gently tugged her towards her him until she was flush against his pelvis, her stomach doing a complete flip turn when she encountered the ridge of his growing erection. She lowered her lashes as his mouth came down, down, down as if in slow motion.

As soon as Molly felt the imprint of his mouth on

hers, a rush of sensation spiralled through her. His kiss was light at first, experimental almost, a slow, measured discovery of the landscape of her lips. He gradually increased the pressure but he didn't deepen the kiss. But somehow it was all the more intimate for that.

He cupped her face in his hands, his lean, long fingers gentle on her cheeks. It was a tender gesture that made her insides melt. She felt the rasp of his unshaven jaw against her chin as he shifted position. It was a spine-tingling reminder of all the essential differences between them: smooth and rough, hard and soft, male and female.

He gently stroked his tongue along the seam of her mouth. It wasn't a command for entry but a tempting lure to make her come in search of him. She pushed the tip of her tongue forward, her whole body quivering when it came into contact with his—male against female. It made fireworks explode inside her body. It unleashed something needy and urgent inside her. She gave a little whimper as his tongue touched hers again, a stab and retreat that had an unmistakably sexual intent about it.

Molly pressed herself closer, her insides clenching with desire as she felt his erection so hot and hard against her belly. His tongue glided against hers, calling it into a circling, whirling dance that made her senses spin like a top.

Had she ever been kissed like this?

Not in this lifetime.

He increased the pressure of his mouth on hers, interspersed with gentle but sexy thrusts and glides of his tongue. His hands slid up into her hair, his fingers splaying out over her scalp where every hair shaft was shivering and quaking in delight.

He broke the kiss to pull at her lips with his mouth, teasing little tugs that made her belly flip and then flop. Then he caressed her lips with a slow, drugging sweep of his tongue before covering her mouth again in a kiss that had a hint of desperation to it.

Molly felt her bones turn to liquid as his mouth worked its mesmerising magic on hers. She had never felt so turned on by a kiss. Hot darts of need pierced her. Her breasts felt tight and sensitive where they were pressing against his chest. Her inner core was moist and aching with that hollow feeling of want that nothing but sex could assuage. She moved her lower body against him, loving the feel of him responding to her so powerfully.

He took a deep breath and pulled back, holding her with his hands on her upper arms. 'We need to stop,' he said, breathing raggedly. '*I* need to stop.'

'Right…of course…good idea. We definitely should stop,' Molly said, suddenly embarrassed at how passionately she had responded to him. Would he think her too easy? Too forward? That was ironic as she was quite possibly the most conservative lover on the planet. But somehow he had unlocked a part of her she hadn't known existed.

He dropped his hold and rubbed at his face with both of his hands. 'I knew this was going to happen. I'm sorry. It's my fault. I was the one who crossed the line. It won't happen again.'

'We kissed,' she said, trying to be all modern and laid back about it. 'What's the big deal?'

His expression tightened. 'This is not just about a kiss and you damn well know it.' He moved to the other side of the kitchen. 'I don't need this right now.'

'Maybe this is just what you need,' Molly said. 'You're too focussed on work. That's why you can't sleep. You haven't got an off button.'

'Don't tell me how to live my life.'

'You're not living your life, though, are you?' she said.

His brows snapped together. 'What's that supposed to mean?'

'You have no life,' Molly said. 'You work ninety-to a hundred-hour weeks. You bite people's heads off. You push people away. You can't even remember the last time you got close to someone.'

'I had sex three months ago.'

Molly arched her brow. 'On your own or with someone?'

He rolled his eyes. 'With a woman I met at a conference.'

'Did you see her more than once?'

'There was no point,' he said. 'The chemistry wasn't right.'

'So it was a one-night stand.'

'There's nothing wrong with a one-night stand as long as it's safe.'

'And you like to be safe, don't you, Lucas?' Molly said. 'Safe from feeling anything for anyone. Safe from having anyone feel anything for you.'

She could see the tension in him. It was in every line and contour of his face. It was in the set of his shoulders and the tight clench of his fists. She could even feel it in the air. It made the atmosphere crackle like scrunched-up baking paper. 'What are you trying to do, Molly?' he asked. 'Push me until I lose control?'

She stepped up to within an inch of his body. His nostrils flared like those of a wild stallion as her scent came to him. Her breasts almost touched his chest. He held himself rigid, every muscle on his face set in stone, his body a marble statue. 'This is what you're frightened of, isn't it, Lucas?' she said as she placed a hand on his chest where his heart was thumping. 'Wanting someone. *Needing* them.'

He covered her hand with his and pulled it off his chest, the strength and grip of his fingers making her wince. 'I want you out of here by the end of the week,' he said, dropping her hand as if it was poisonous.

'Why?' she asked. 'Because you don't like letting someone see how incredibly lonely you are when you haven't got work to distract you?'

His jaw looked like it had been set in concrete. 'If you're not careful I'll throw you out tonight.'

'I don't think you mean that,' Molly said.

'You want to put it to the test?' he asked.

She looked at the steely glint in his eyes and backed down. 'Not particularly.'

'Wise of you,' he said.

'I'm only doing it because of Mittens,' she said. 'If it wasn't for him, I would've left before this.'

'You shouldn't have come in the first place.'

'You invited me!'

'I meant to London,' he said. 'You should have known it would cause trouble. But that's probably why you came. You could destroy my reputation with a word to the right person and you damn well know it.'

Molly frowned as she looked at him. 'I didn't realise you had such an appalling opinion of me. Do you really think that's why I'm here?'

'I've paid for what happened to your brother,' he said. 'Every day of my life since I have paid for that error of judgement. I can't bring him back. I can't undo what's done. I just want to be left to get on with my life. Is that too much to ask?'

'But you're not getting on with your life,' Molly said. 'You're stuck. Just like I'm stuck. Matt haunts us both. We both feel guilty.'

'You have no need to feel guilty,' he said. 'You weren't driving the car that killed him.'

'Why did you go out that night?'

He closed his eyes as if trying to block out the memory. 'I didn't want to go,' he said. 'Matt was pretty wired. He was in one of those moods he got into from time to time. I didn't find out until later that he'd been grounded, otherwise I wouldn't have agreed to go. But he always wanted to push the boundaries. He wanted the adrenalin rush. That's why I insisted on getting back behind the wheel. I thought he was being reckless. I didn't mind going for a drive to hang out, but doing tailspins and doughnuts wasn't my thing. I didn't see the kangaroo until it was too late. If I'd had more experience or if we'd been in a later model car, I would probably have handled it better. I lost control on the gravel. I didn't even realise he hadn't done up his seat belt until I saw him hit the windscreen.'

'Matt wouldn't have gone out at all if it hadn't been for me,' Molly said.

'What do you mean?' he asked.

'I found his stash of cigarettes and told my parents,' she said. 'That's why they grounded him. He was upset with me about it. I've always blamed myself for what happened. I wish I'd kept my mouth shut.'

Lucas frowned. 'You were just a little kid,' he said. 'You did the right thing. Matt shouldn't have been smoking, especially as he had asthma. He stole those cigarettes from Hagley's store. I was furious with him about it. But he was always pulling pranks like that.'

Molly let her shoulders drop on a sigh. 'I can't help blaming myself. Not just about Matt, but about my parents. Once he was gone…I wasn't enough for them. I couldn't make them happy. I couldn't keep our family together no matter how hard I tried.'

He came over to her and placed a gentle hand on her shoulder. 'Your parents were having trouble well before Matt's death,' he said. 'He told me about it heaps of times. You might not have noticed, being so much younger. Young kids tend to see what they want to see. Matt was sure your parents were heading for a break-up. His death probably just postponed it for a few years.'

Molly looked up into his face. His eyes were kind, his touch so gentle it made her melt all over again. 'I've never really talked to anyone about this before,' she said. 'Everybody always clammed up as soon as I came into the room. It was like the mere mention of Matt's name would damage me in some way. I guess they thought they were protecting me, but in the long run it made it so much harder. I had no one to talk to about him, about how much I missed him, about how guilty I felt. It must have been like that for you too.'

His expression spasmed in pain as he dropped his hand from her shoulder. 'It was one of the worst things about the whole tragedy,' he said. 'I lost my best mate and then no one would ever talk to me about him. My parents did their best but they didn't want to upset me. My brothers didn't know how to handle it. It was as if Matt had never existed.'

'I don't think Matt would want us to keep punishing ourselves for what happened,' Molly said. 'He would want us to be happy—to get on with our lives. Can't you see that?'

'I'm not going to take advantage of you,' he said, his mouth flattening in resolve. 'You're a long way from home. You're way out of your depth. You're uncertain about your relationship with Simon whatever his name is. I'm not going to add to your confusion by conducting an affair with you that will only end in tears.'

'It doesn't have to end in tears,' she said. 'We could have a great relationship. We have a lot in common. We have the same values. We have the same background.'

He gave her a bleak look. 'How long do you think a relationship between us would last?' he asked. 'Your parents would be up in arms about it. It would devastate them. It would devastate my own parents. Do you think they haven't suffered enough? They've paid a high price for my mistake. I won't have them suffer anything else.'

'You're wrong, Lucas,' Molly said. 'It wouldn't devastate them. It might actually help them, and my parents too. Can't you see that? It would help them to realise life goes on. We could help them heal.'

'I can't do it,' he said. 'I *won't* do it. You're not think-ing straight. You're caught up with the nostalgic notion of me being your brother's best friend. That's all it is, Molly. You're not attracted to me for any other reason.'

'This is not about Matt,' Molly said. 'This is about us.'

'There is no us without Matt,' he said. 'Can't you see that? He's a shadow that will always be over us. You will always see me as the person who was responsible for his death. I get that. I totally understand and accept it because it's true. But I don't want to spend the rest of my life being reminded of it. Every time I look at you I see Matt. Every time you look at me you see the man who tore your family apart. How long do you think a relationship with that sort of backstory will last?'

'There is such a thing as moving on,' Molly said. 'We can't change the past but we can move on from it.'

'I'm sorry, Molly,' he said. 'You're a sweet girl. You're exactly the sort of girl I used to think I would one day settle down with. But that was then, this is now. I don't want to complicate my life with emotional entanglements.'

'There will come a day when work won't be enough any more,' she said. 'What will you do then?'

He gave her a wry look. 'I'll get myself a cat.'

'Funny.'

'That's me,' he said. 'A laugh a minute.'

'You're never going to allow yourself to be happy, are you?' Molly said. 'This is the hair shirt you've cho-sen—to live the rest of your life without love and con-nection. But it's not going to bring Matt back. It's not going to do anything but make you and the people who love you miserable. I feel sorry for you. You're like a tiger in a paper cage. You're the only one who can free yourself but you're too stubborn to do it.'

'Why are you so interested in my happiness?' he asked. 'You're the last person who should be worrying about how I feel.'

'You're not a bad person, Lucas,' Molly said. 'You just had a bad thing happen to you. You need to forgive yourself for being human.'

He touched her on the cheek with a slow stroke of his finger. 'Sweet, caring little Molly,' he said. 'You've always had a soft little heart. Always rescuing lame ducks and hopeless cases and getting yourself hurt in the process.'

She looked into his hazel eyes as tears welled in her own. 'I don't know how to live any other way.'

He leaned down and pressed a soft kiss to the middle of her forehead as if she were ten years old. 'Go back to bed,' he said. 'I'll see you in the morning.'

Molly slipped out of the room but it was a long time before she heard him make his way upstairs.

CHAPTER SIX

LUCAS WAS RECALIBRATING Tim Merrick's respirator the following morning and talking Catriona, one of the more junior nurses, through it. 'The pressure has gone up, which indicates pulmonary oedema,' he said. 'This means the lungs are stiff, and the ventilator pressure has to be turned up to inflate the lungs and get enough oxygen on board to give the brain the best chance of recovery. If the oxygen level in the blood drops, the brain damage will worsen instead of improve.'

'Is he likely to recover?' Catriona asked with a concerned look.

'We're doing all we can to make sure he does,' he said. *Don't die. Don't die. Don't die.* It was like a chant he couldn't get out of his head.

He had visited young Hamish on the ward first thing this morning. It was like looking at himself seventeen years ago. Hamish had the same hollow look of anguish in his eyes, the same shocked, this-can't-be-happening expression on his face. It was gut-wrenching to witness. It brought back his own anguish and guilt in great swamping waves.

Lucas turned to the nurse again. 'Can you run some blood gases through the analyser? I've got inflation pressure up another notch and oxygen is on one hundred per cent. I'm going to administer some frusemide to increase urine output to try and dry out the lungs a bit.'

A few minutes later Catriona called the readings out to Lucas.

'Damn,' he said. 'He's getting respiratory acidosis and we still haven't got the O2 up.'

'The X-ray's here for his chest film, Lucas,' Molly said as she came over.

'Maybe that will show something reversible,' he said. 'If we can't get that oxygen level up then the chance of recovery is going to slip away. Hypoxia and cerebral oedema is a bad combination.'

They looked at the images on the screen. 'You still think he's going to make it?' she asked.

Lucas stripped off his gloves, tossed them in the bin and walked over to the lightbox. 'It's still too early to say with any certainty,' he said. 'It might be a couple of weeks or more before that swelling goes down.'

'He's got a decerebrate posture—the clawed hands,' Molly said. 'I can't imagine how his parents must be feeling, to see him like that.'

'Emma Wingfield looked as bad at this stage, if not worse,' he said. 'Young brains have a knack of beating the odds and recovering. By the time people are admitted here with a tube in every orifice even their relatives don't recognise them. A few months later they'll walk in here with a box of chocolates—you'd never have guessed it was them under all that technology.' *He just hoped Tim was going to another one of them.*

'He's got a big effusion on the right,' Molly said.

'Yeah,' he said, looking at it. 'That's definitely worth draining. Might significantly improve lung function.'

Su Ling came across. 'Dr Banning?' she said. 'We've got a response from Claire Mitchell.'

Lucas called to Aleem, who was coming in with blood reports. 'Can you get set up here for me to do a drain?' To Molly he said, 'Come with me. It'll take half an hour for him to set up. I could use you over here.'

'What's happened?' he asked, when they got to Claire's bed.

'She's opened her eyes and she's fighting the ventilator,' Su Ling said.

It was the best news Lucas had had all day, maybe all year. 'Talk to her, Molly, while I look at the pressure.'

'Claire, can you hear me? It's Dr Drummond,' Molly said gently. 'You've had an accident and you're in Intensive Care. You're going to be all right. We've got you on a machine to help you breathe.'

'Her intracranial pressure's through the roof,' Lucas said. 'It's good she's responding but we're going to have to sedate her to get the pressure down. We need a few more days to wean her off the supports.'

'I'll give ten IV diazepam and up the sedation for twenty-four hours,' Molly said.

'Good,' he said. 'Another twenty-four hours and we'll turn down the sedation, see if she's less agitated and the IC pressure doesn't go up so much. I'll go and have a word with her parents. Are they here?'

'They left just half an hour ago to grab a coffee,' Su Ling said. 'They won't be long.'

'Right,' he said. 'I'll do that drain first.'

'I can do the drain,' Molly said, swinging her gaze to his. 'You can't do everything all at once.'

She had a point but Lucas wasn't going to let her know it. 'Call me if you have any difficulties,' he said, and left to find Claire's parents.

'Dr Drummond,' Jacqui said as Molly came into the office after a break later that day. 'This is Emma Wingfield. She's a previous inmate of ours. Emma, this is Dr Drummond. She's from Australia, like Dr Banning.'

'Hello,' Molly said with a smile. 'I've been hearing wonderful things about you. Dr Banning told me you were one of his star patients.'

Emma blushed, making her look far younger than nineteen. 'I owe him my life. He's the most amazing man.' She held out a plastic container. 'I've made him brownies. They're his favourite. Is he here? I'd love a quick word with him.'

'I don't think he's back from a meeting with the CEO,' Jacqui said, glancing up at the clock. 'It's been a pretty crazy day around here. He was late leaving so the meeting will probably run overtime.'

'That's OK,' Emma said. 'I'll wait. That is if I'm not in the way?'

'Not at all,' Jacqui said. 'Why don't you take a seat in one of the counselling rooms and I'll get him to come to you as soon as he gets back?'

Emma tucked the brownie container under one arm and left with another shy smile.

Jacqui turned and looked at Molly. 'I didn't have the heart to tell her you were living with Lucas,' she said. 'Her first real crush. Don't you just ache for her?'

Molly felt a blush steal over her cheeks not unlike the one young Emma had just experienced. 'I told you I'm not involved with him. I'm just sharing his house temporarily.'

'Yeah, but I've got two eyes in my head,' Jacqui said. 'He can barely take his eyes off you and you blush every time he walks into the room. So what gives? What's the deal with you guys? Did you have a fling in the past or something?'

'No, of course not,' Molly said. 'I was just a kid when he left to come over here.'

Jacqui tapped her finger against her lips. 'But there's something between you, isn't there?'

Molly gave a little sigh. 'He and my older brother were best friends,' she said, hoping to fob her off.

'Ah, now I get it,' Jacqui said. 'Lucas thinks your brother wouldn't approve of him making a move on his kid sister. That's typical of him, ever the gentleman. So what does your brother do? Is he a doctor too?'

'Um…no.' She paused for a moment before continuing, 'He died a while back. A car accident.'

'I'm so sorry,' Jacqui said. 'How dreadful for you and your family. And for Lucas too, to lose a best mate.'

'Yes…yes, it was dreadful,' Molly said. 'But it was an accident. It wasn't anyone's fault. It was just one of those things.'

Jacqui looked past Molly's left shoulder. 'Ah, here he is now,' she said as Lucas came in. 'You have a visitor— Emma Wingfield. She's waiting in one of the counselling rooms. She's brought you brownies.'

'Right.' Lucas gave a brisk nod and walked back out again.

Jacqui rolled her eyes. 'One of us should probably tell him,' she said. 'You know what men are like. You have to hit them over the head with something before they see it.'

Molly chewed at her lip. 'I'll have a word with him later.'

Molly found him in his office, going through some journals at the end of the day. 'Can I have a quick word?' she asked from the door.

'Sure,' he said, placing the journal he'd been reading to one side. 'What's up?'

She rolled her lips together to moisten them. 'Um… it's about Emma.'

He frowned. 'Emma?'

'Emma Wingfield.'

'What about her?'

Molly shifted her weight from foot to foot, feeling a little out of her depth and uncertain. Maybe she should have got Jacqui to say something. Would he misread her motives for bringing Emma's infatuation to his attention? 'I may be speaking out of turn but I couldn't help noticing she's rather attached to you,' she said.

His eyes held hers steady. 'And your point is?'

She felt her cheeks fire up. 'She's very young. You should be careful you don't give her the wrong idea. She could get very hurt.'

'I was her doctor, for God's sake,' he said. 'Anyway, she's just a kid.'

'She's nineteen, almost twenty,' Molly said. 'That's old enough to have a relationship with a man who is technically no longer her doctor.'

'I'm not having a relationship with her,' he said. 'She comes in from time to time to say hi to all the staff who looked after her. I told you that the other day.'

'She only wanted to see you today,' Molly said. 'She barely said a word to anyone else. I think she fancies herself in love with you.'

'That's rubbish,' he said. 'Why would she be in love with me?'

'You're handsome and kind and you saved her life,' Molly said. 'That's just for starters. I'm sure there are a hundred reasons why she has a crush on you. Just about every single woman at St Patrick's fancies you like crazy so why should she be any different?'

His eyes measured hers for a pulsing moment. 'Why indeed?'

Molly knew her cheeks were bright red but carried on regardless. 'I think you need to let her down gently. She's young and vulnerable. She's been through a traumatic experience and is still finding her way.'

'Emma wants to do something for the unit,' he said. 'Some fundraising. That's why she wanted to meet with me as unit director. I said I'd help her do something. I'm not sure what. We're still at the brainstorming stage. Maybe you could offer some suggestions. I haven't got a clue about that sort of thing.'

'I'd be happy to help,' Molly said. 'I was involved in a dinner dance for our unit back home. It was a great success. Everyone talked about it for months afterwards.'

'I'll arrange a meeting between the two of you to get things rolling,' he said.

'I still think you should be careful in handling Emma,' Molly said. 'I'm sure her reasons for the fundraising are very noble, but you still have to keep in mind she could be actively seeking time alone with you.'

'Thanks for the tip-off,' he said. 'But I'm sure you're mistaken. Anyway, I think she already has a boyfriend.'

'Yes, well, that doesn't always signify,' Molly said.

His brow came up in an arc. 'Are you speaking from experience?'

'Not necessarily.'

'How is Simon what's-his-name?' he asked. 'I saw him chatting up one of the young midwives in the cafeteria this afternoon. He sure gets around, doesn't he?'

'He's a free agent,' Molly said. 'He can chat up whoever he likes.'

'So you're no longer an item?'

'We weren't really one in the first place,' she said, blowing out a breath. 'I was what you'd call a rebound fill-in for him. I was feeling a bit lonely at the time but now I wish I'd never let him cry on my shoulder. I can see why his ex left him. He's quite narcissistic and controlling.'

'And possessive.'

'That too.'

There was a little silence.

'I might be a bit late coming home this evening,' Molly said. 'I'm going to a movie night with Kate Harrison's group. I was…um, wondering if you'd like to come too.'

'Why would I want to do that?' he asked.

'It would be good for you,' she said, 'to take your mind off work for a change. Things have been pretty stressful what with Tim Merrick and all. I thought it'd be nice to get out and socialise a bit so—'

'I already have an engagement this evening.'

'Doing what?'

'Do you really want me to spell it out for you?' he asked with a sardonic quirk of his brow.

Molly blushed. 'Oh, right... Sorry, I didn't mean to embarrass you or anything...'

He picked up his journal again. 'Close the door on the way out, will you?'

CHAPTER SEVEN

MOLLY WAS DISTRACTED all the way through the movie. She couldn't stop thinking about what Lucas was up to and who he might be with tonight. Who was it? She didn't think it was anyone from the hospital. She felt agitated at the thought of him bringing someone back to his house.

What if his lady friend spent the night? She herself would no doubt encounter her in the morning. It would be beyond embarrassing. It would be heart-breaking to see him with someone else. She couldn't handle it. She didn't want to handle it. She hated the thought of some woman coming back just to sleep with him. Would they be interested in who he was as a person? Would they take the time to get to know him? To understand what had made him the quiet, reserved man he was?

Of course not.

He wouldn't allow them to. He had let no one into his private world of pain. He shouldered his guilt and anguish with dogged determination. He had no joy in his life, or at least none that she could see. He was isolated and deeply lonely but he wouldn't allow anyone to get close to him.

Molly didn't join the others for drinks after the

movie. She caught a cab back to Lucas's house and went inside with an ear out for the sound of voices, but it was as silent as a tomb. She checked the sitting room but it didn't look like anyone had even been in there. The cushions on the sofa were all still neatly arranged. The coffee table was neat with its glossy book of iconic photographs from around the world centred just so. There were no condensation rings from drinks or crumbs from nibbles.

Maybe he'd decided to stay at his date's place, or maybe he'd booked a hotel room, she thought in stomach-plummeting despair. She didn't want him to make love to someone who didn't know him, who didn't care for him...*who didn't love him.*

Molly was about to head upstairs after feeding and playing with Mittens when the front door opened and Lucas came in, bringing a waft of chilly air with him.

'How was your date?' she asked.

'I had to take a rain-check,' he said as he shrugged himself out of his jacket. 'I got a call from the hospital. Tim Merrick's temperature suddenly skyrocketed. He started leaking CSF from one ear.'

'Oh, no...' Molly frowned in concern. Leaking cerebrospinal fluid and a fever probably meant meningitis had occurred. The damage to his brain could increase if it wasn't quickly controlled.

'It's a setback,' he said. 'But I hope we've caught it in time.'

Molly watched as he rubbed a hand across the back of his neck. He grimaced as if his muscles were in knots. 'You look tired,' she said.

'Yeah, well, eighteen-hour days do that.'

'I could massage your neck for you if you like,' she offered.

'You'd break your fingers working on my golf balls of tension,' he said. 'I'll be fine. I just need a couple of hours' sleep.'

'I'd like to do it for you,' Molly said. 'It won't take long. I'm pretty good at it. I used to do my dad's neck and shoulders all the time.'

He looked at her for a long moment. 'You sure you want to get that close to me?' he asked.

'Will you bite if I do?' she asked with an arch look.

'Guess there's only one way to find out,' he said.

A few minutes later Molly had him sitting on one of the sofas in the sitting room. She stood behind him and started kneading his neck through his shirt. His muscles felt like concrete and his shirt wasn't helping matters as it kept bunching up. 'I think you'd better take your shirt off,' she said. 'I can't get into those muscles the way I want to.'

'It's been a while since a woman's asked me to strip for her,' he said as he unbuttoned his shirt.

'Ha ha,' Molly said. 'Now, stay put while I get some massage oil.'

When she came back with some perfumed oil he was sitting bare chested on the sofa. She drank in the sight of his broad tanned shoulders and the leanness of his corded muscles. She poured some oil into her hand and emulsified it before placing her hands on his shoulder.

'I'm sorry if my hands are cold,' she said. 'It won't take long to warm them up.'

'They're fine,' he said with a little groan. 'Perfect.'

'You're so tense.'

'You should feel it from my side.'

Molly smiled and kept massaging. She loved the feel of his warm male skin underneath her hands. After a while he started to relax. She worked on his neck muscles right up to his scalp, turning his head to the right and then to the left to loosen the tension.

'You missed your calling,' he said.

'When was the last time you had a massage?' she asked as she worked on his scalp with her fingertips.

'Can't remember.'

Molly kept stroking and gliding her hands over his shoulders. Over time the movements of her hands became less vigorous and more like caresses. She breathed in the musky scent of him as she worked her way down over his pectoral muscles. She heard him draw in a breath as her fingers skated over the top of his abdomen. It was daring and brazen of her but she couldn't leave it at that. She inched her way down, taking her time, stroking each horizontal ridge of toned male flesh.

The air became loaded with sensual intent as she found the cave of his belly button surrounded by its nest of coarse masculine hair.

He suddenly captured her hand and stilled it against the rock-hard wall of his stomach. 'Molly.' His voice was as rusty as an old hinge.

'Yes?'

He pushed her hand away and got to his feet, turning to face her across the sofa, his eyes dark and full of glittering desire. 'What the hell are you playing at?' he asked.

'I was massaging you.'

'The hell you were,' he said. 'Do you have any idea

how hard this is for me? Do you think I don't want you? Of course I do. I can't think of a time when I've wanted someone more.'

'Then why are you fighting it?'

He flicked his eyes upwards as he turned away. 'For God's sake, you know why.'

Molly came from behind the sofa to stand in front of him. 'No, I don't know why,' she said. 'We're both adults. There's no reason we can't have a relationship. This has nothing to do with anyone else but us.'

He dragged a hand over his face in a weary fashion. 'I can't promise you a future because of the past. The past *I'm* responsible for.'

'We can make the future *in spite* of the past,' Molly countered. 'Haven't we both suffered enough? Why should we spend the rest of our lives grieving over what we've lost instead of celebrating what we still have?'

'It will always be there between us,' he said. 'It won't go away. It will fester in the background until one day it will blow up in our faces. I can't risk that.'

'Life is full of risks,' she said. 'You can't protect yourself from every one of them. Loving and losing are part of what a rich human life entails.'

'I lost everything when Matt died,' he said heavily. 'I lost my best mate. I lost my family. My community. The future I'd envisaged for myself. It was all gone in the blink of an eye.'

'So you're going to punish yourself for the rest of your life because you don't feel you deserve to be happy?' Molly asked. 'But what about my happiness?'

He closed his eyes briefly. 'I can't make you happy.'

'You're not even prepared to give it a try, are you?' she asked. 'You've made up your mind. You're going to live a life of self-sacrifice. But it won't achieve anything. All it will do is make you end up lonely and isolated. Pretty much as you are now. You're jammed on replay. Lonely, lonely, lonely.'

He gave her an irritated look. 'I'm not lonely. I like being alone. I don't need people around me all the time.'

Molly rolled her eyes and turned away. 'Good luck with that.'

He snagged her arm and turned her back to face him. 'What's that supposed to mean?'

She gave him a direct look. 'Why did you ask me to stay here with you?'

'You needed a place to stay in a hurry,' he said. 'I couldn't see you tossed out on the street. I wasn't brought up that way.'

'I think you asked me to stay with you because deep down you're tired of being alone,' Molly said. 'You're sick of rattling around in this big old house with no one to talk to. The occasional dates and one-night stands aren't cutting it any more. You're yearning for something more meaningful.'

'You're wrong,' he said, snatching up his shirt and shoving his arms through the sleeves.

'Am I?'

'I don't need to be rescued, Molly,' he said, glowering at her. 'I'm not going to be another one of your lame-duck projects. Find someone else to rehabilitate.' He turned and strode out of the room, closing the door with a snap behind him.

* * *

Over the next few days Molly only saw Lucas at work.
He barely seemed to spend any time at home at all. He
left in the morning before she got up and he came back
when she was already tucked up in bed. She didn't know
when he ate or slept. She found herself listening out for
him at all hours of the night, not really settling until
she heard him come up the stairs and close his bedroom
door. He drove himself relentlessly. She wondered how
long he could keep doing it. The job was demanding at
the best of times, but he had taken on extra shifts as if
work was all he wanted to do.

Molly had the weekend off and spent it shopping and
sightseeing. But on Sunday night she felt at a loose end.
She hadn't seen Lucas all weekend, although she had
noticed he had fed Mittens and cleaned his litter tray.

After watching a movie she wasn't really interested
in, Molly took a long soak in the bath before preparing for bed. She spent a couple of hours trying to relax
enough to go to sleep but she kept jolting awake when
she thought she heard Lucas's key in the lock.

Finally, at three in the morning, she gave up and
came back downstairs for a drink. On her way back up
she noticed there was a light on in the library. It seemed
she wasn't the only one having trouble sleeping. She
padded to the door, which was ajar, and gently pushed
it open. Lucas was sitting on the comfortable sofa in
the middle of the room with his head resting against
the back, his long legs stretched out in front of him,
crossed at the ankles. His book was lying open on his
lap and his eyes were closed, as if he had fallen asleep
in mid-sentence.

He looked much younger in sleep. His features were less harshly drawn and the normally grim set of his mouth was relaxed. His hair was tousled as if his hands had been moving through it, and his shirt was crumpled and the first three buttons undone, showing a glimpse of his sternum.

She walked over to him but still he didn't stir. She watched his chest rise and fall on each slow and even breath. After a moment she carefully took the book from his lap and placed it on the nearby side table.

Still he slept.

Molly reached out with her hand and ever so gently brushed a lock of hair off his forehead. His eyelids flickered momentarily but didn't open. He made a small murmuring noise and let out another long exhalation.

She picked up the throw rug that was draped over the end of the sofa and gently spread it over him.

He didn't stir.

She touched his face with her fingertips. His stubble caught on her soft skin like silk on coarse-grade sandpaper. She sent her fingertip on an even more daring journey to trace over his top lip and then his bottom one. His lips were dry and warm and so very, very tempting...

She hesitated for a moment before she leaned down and pressed a soft-as-air kiss to his mouth. His much dryer lips clung to hers as she gently pulled back. But then he gave a little start and opened his eyes, his hands wrapping around hers like a snare captured a rabbit.

'I was just...making sure you were warm enough,' she said.

For a moment he said nothing. Did nothing. Just sat

there with his eyes meshed with hers, his warm strong hands holding hers captive.

The silence swelled with sensual promise.

'I didn't mean to wake you…' Molly said. 'You looked so…peaceful.'

He gave her hands a gentle little tug to bring her down beside him on the sofa. 'Why aren't you in bed?' he asked.

'I couldn't sleep.'

His eyes moved over her face as if he was memorising every tiny detail. He paused longest on her mouth. 'Isn't it the handsome prince who's supposed to kiss Sleeping Beauty to get her to wake up?' he asked.

Molly moistened her lips with a quick dart of the tip of her tongue. 'Yes, but I'm already awake so what would be the point?'

His eyes smouldered as they came back to hers. 'This thing between us…it's not going to go away, is it?'

'Not in this lifetime.'

A corner of his mouth lifted.

'Hey, you almost smiled,' she said, touching his lip with her finger.

He captured her finger with his mouth and sucked on it erotically while his gaze held hers. Molly felt her stomach drop. The sexy graze of his teeth and the rasp of his tongue made her shiver with delight. He tugged her closer, a gentle but determined tug that had a primal element to it. His eyes were dark with desire as he pressed her down against the cushioned sofa, his long lean body a delicious, tantalising weight on her.

His eyes made love with hers for endless seconds. 'I told myself I wasn't going to do this,' he said.

Molly looped her arms around his neck. 'I want you to do this,' she said. 'And I'm pretty sure you want to do this too.'

His mouth tilted wryly. 'I guess I can't really deny that right now, can I?'

She moved against the hard press of his erection. 'Not a chance.'

He brought his mouth down and covered hers in a hungry kiss. It was a kiss of longing and desperation, a kiss that spoke of deep yearnings that hadn't been satisfied for a long, long time. His tongue stroked the seam of her mouth to gain access, thrusting between her lips to meet her tongue in a sexy tangle. Molly clasped his head in her hands, her fingers threading through his hair as he worked his sensual magic on her mouth. Her breasts were tingling against the hard wall of his chest, her pelvis on fire where his erection probed her boldly.

One of his hands lifted her hips to bring her even harder against him. She gave a little gasp of pleasure as his other hand cupped her breast through her wrap. But it wasn't enough for him. He tugged open the wrap and went in search of her naked flesh. She shivered as he bent his head to suckle on her. Her nipple was sensitive and tightly budded but he seemed to know exactly what pressure to subject it to. He swirled his tongue around her areole before moving to the exquisitely reactive underside of her breast. He kissed and stroked and suckled in turn, until she was almost breathless with want.

Molly pushed his shirt back off his shoulders, smoothing her hands over the muscled planes of his chest, delighting in the feel of him, so hard and warm and male. He groaned as she slid her hands down over his taut abdomen, his kiss becoming more and more urgent against her mouth. She wriggled out of her wrap and then set to work on the waistband of his trousers. She finally uncovered him, stroking and cupping him until he was breathing as hard as she was. He was gloriously aroused, thick and swollen, hot to her touch, already moist at the tip. She rubbed the pad of her thumb over him, her insides quivering when he gave a low, deep groan of pleasure.

After a moment or two he pulled her hand away and pressed her harder back against the sofa cushions. He kissed his way down her body, lingering over her breasts, down to her belly button, dipping in there with his tongue before moving to the feminine heart of her.

Molly drew in a sharp breath as his warm breath skated over her sensitive folds. She clutched at his head, her fingers digging in for purchase when his tongue gently separated her. 'I don't usually do this...' she said. 'Can we just...? Oh...*oh*...' She closed her eyes as the delicious sensations barrelled through her like a set of turbulent waves. Once it had subsided she opened her eyes and looked at Lucas, suddenly feeling shy. 'That was...amazing... I've never let anyone do that before.'

He leaned his weight on his elbows as he looked down at her. 'You haven't?'

She shook her head. 'I've always felt a bit uncomfortable about it. I know this sounds ridiculous but it always seemed a bit too intimate.'

He brushed back her hair from her forehead. 'You probably weren't with the right partner,' he said. 'Trust is just as important as lust.'

'Speaking of lust…' She stroked her fingers over his erection. 'Don't you want to…?'

'I haven't got a condom on me right now,' he said.

'Do you have any upstairs?' she asked.

'A couple maybe.'

Molly caressed his lean jaw with her fingers. She was used to men who were *always* prepared. 'Let's go upstairs,' she whispered softly.

Lucas carried her in his arms, stopping now and again to kiss her deeply and passionately. Finally he laid her on his bed and came down over her, his weight balanced on his arms so as not to crush her. Molly lifted her hips towards his, her whole body aching and yearning for his deep possession.

He kissed her lingeringly, moving from her mouth to her breasts and back again until she was whimpering and writhing. She clawed at him with her hands, digging her fingers into his buttocks to hold him close to the pulsing heat of her body.

He paused for a moment to apply a condom, and came back over her, his strong thighs imprisoning hers. His first thrust was gentle, almost tentative, as if he was uncertain of whether or not to proceed. But her body gripped him hungrily and with a deep groan of pleasure he surged forward, again and again and again. Molly clung to him as the delicious friction sent her nerves into a frenzy of excitement. He went deeper, his breathing harsh against her neck as he fought for control, his lean, athletic body taut as a bow with the build-up of tension. She caressed his back and shoulders with her hands, feeling the gravel of goose-bumps break out along his skin as he responded to her touch.

He slipped a hand between their rocking bodies to find her most pleasurable point as he continued his rhythmic thrusts. The touch of his fingers, so gentle, so intuitive, triggered her orgasm within seconds. It was like a tumultuous wave that tossed and turned her over and over and over until she was gasping and sobbing with the aftershocks. She had never felt such powerful, all-consuming sensations before. Her body reverberated with them as he laboured towards his own release. She held him tightly against her as he finally let go. She felt every deep pumping action inside her, heard his desperate groan, a primal sound that made her shiver all over in feminine response.

Molly held him to her, unwilling to break the intimate connection. To lie there with his body still encased in hers, to have his arms hold her close, to feel the rise and fall of his chest against hers as his breathing gradually slowed, was too precious, too special to sever just yet.

'I'm sorry if I rushed you,' he said against her neck where his head was resting.

She toyed with his hair with her fingers. 'You didn't,' she said. 'It was perfect.'

He lifted himself up on one elbow to mesh his gaze with hers. It was hard to know what he was thinking. His expression wasn't shuttered but neither was it totally open. 'I guess I should let you get to bed and get some sleep,' he said.

Molly felt a little frown pucker her forehead. 'You don't want me to stay here with you?'

He eased himself away and dealt with the disposal of

the condom, his eyes not meeting hers. 'I'm a restless sleeper,' he said. 'I'll disturb you too much.'

She watched him as he shrugged on a bathrobe, but the thick terry towelling fabric was not the only barrier he had put up. A mask had slipped over his face as well.

'I guess I'd better get out of your hair, then,' Molly said, and got off the bed, taking the top sheet with her to cover her nakedness. Hurt coursed through her like a poison. How could he dismiss her like that? As if she was a call girl who had served her purpose and now he wanted her gone. She had expected more—*wanted* more—from him. Tears prickled and burned behind her eyes as she shuffled to the door in her makeshift covering, almost tripping over the fringe of the Persian rug.

'Molly.'

She held herself stiffly, with her arms wrapped around her middle as she faced him. 'I can see why your sex life has been experiencing a bit of a downturn,' she said. 'Your bedside manner definitely needs some work.'

He put a hand through his hair, a frown carving deep in his forehead. 'I'm sorry,' he said. 'It wasn't my intention to hurt you.' He dropped his hand back by his side. 'Tonight was…perfect. I mean that, Molly. *You* were perfect.'

She let out a long, exasperated sigh. 'Then why are you pushing me away?'

He held her look for a long moment. 'This is all I can give you,' he said. 'You have to understand and accept that. I know it's not what you want in a relationship but it's all I can give right now.'

'Just…sex?' she asked.

A tiny knot of tension flicked on and off in his jaw. 'Not just sex.'

'But not love and commitment,' she said.

He exhaled a long breath. 'You're only here for three months. It wouldn't be fair to make promises neither of us might be able to keep. Besides, you might feel very differently about things once your parents hear we're involved.'

Molly knew that was going to be a tricky hurdle to cross. For so long she had striven for her father's approval and becoming involved with Lucas was going to destroy any hope of ever achieving that. 'I'm hoping both my parents will put my happiness before any misgivings they might have,' she said. 'Isn't that what most parents want—their kids to be happy?'

'Most, I imagine,' he said.

'How will your parents handle it?'

A shadow passed through his eyes. 'I'm not planning on telling them any time soon.'

Molly couldn't help feeling a little crushed. Did that mean he didn't think they would be involved long enough for his parents to find out? Was he ashamed of his attraction towards her? She bit down on her lip, torn between her pride and her passion for him. Why did it have to be so hard to be happy? Was her life always going to be one of compromise? Of never feeling quite good enough?

Lucas closed the distance between them, tipping up her chin to bring her gaze in line with his. 'I've upset you,' he said.

'Why would you think that?' Molly asked. 'You had sex with me and as soon as it was over you told me to leave. You don't want anyone to know about us being involved. And you can't see us having any sort of future. Why on earth would I be upset?'

He brushed his thumb over her bottom lip, his gaze rueful as it held hers. 'You deserve much better than I could ever give you.'

'But what if I only want you?' she said trying not to cry.

He gathered her close, resting his chin on the top of her head, his warm breath moving through the strands of her hair. 'I have this amazing habit of hurting everyone I care about,' he said.

Molly looked up at him. 'You care about me?'

He held her gaze for an infinitesimal moment. 'Are you going to give my sheet back?' he asked.

'You want it back?'

'Only if you come with it.'

'You'll have to fight me for it,' she said with a coquettish smile.

His eyes smouldered as he reached for the edge of the sheet. 'Game on,' he said, and stripped it from her.

CHAPTER EIGHT

LUCAS WOKE TO find one of Molly's arms flung across his chest, her head snuggled against his side and her slim legs entwined with his. He couldn't remember the last time he had woken up beside someone in his bed. His sexual encounters were normally brief and purely functional. As soon as they were over he forgot about them.

But waking up beside Molly was not going to be something he could so easily dismiss from his memory. The way she had responded to him had been one of the most deeply moving things he had ever experienced. He felt like he was her first lover. In a way she had felt like his. Had he ever felt so fully satiated? So in tune with someone that he forgot where his body ended and hers began? His senses had screamed with delight and they were still humming now hours later. The scent of her perfume was on his skin. Her taste was in his mouth. His hunger for her was stirring his blood all over again.

She moved against him and slowly opened her eyes. 'Hello,' she said with a shy smile.

'Hello to you,' he said as he brushed an imaginary hair off her face.

She traced one of her fingertips over his top lip. 'Last night was wonderful,' She said. '*You* were wonderful.

I've never felt like that before. I've always thought it was my fault, you know, that I wasn't very good at sex. But now I can see what I've been missing out on.'

He caught her hand and kissed the end of her finger. 'It was wonderful for me, too,' he said.

She trailed her fingers over his sternum, her grey-blue eyes lowered from his. 'I guess it's pretty much the same for men, no matter who they have sex with,' she said.

He brought her chin up. 'Not always,' he said. 'I agree that it's often more of a physical thing for men than for women, but caring about someone does make a difference.'

Her eyes shone as she put her arms around his neck. 'Is it time to get up yet?' she asked.

He rolled her beneath him and pinned her with his body. 'Not yet,' he said, and covered her mouth with his.

Molly came downstairs after her shower to find Lucas had already left for the hospital. There was a short note on the kitchen counter to say he would catch up with her later at work. She put the note down and sighed. They hadn't really had time to discuss how they were going to manage their relationship in public.

Was it a relationship? Or had she done the same thing she had done with Simon—drifted into something that didn't have a name?

She knew Lucas was keen to keep his private life separate but she couldn't see how they would be able to stop people finding out they were intimately involved unless he planned to be all formal and distant with her at work. It wasn't that she wanted her private life out on show, but neither did she want to hide her relationship with Lucas away as if she was somehow ashamed of it.

She still couldn't believe how amazing he made her feel. Her body was still tingling from his passionate lovemaking. Every time she moved her body she felt where he had been. Holding him tightly within her as he had come had surpassed anything she had ever experienced before. She had felt so deeply connected to him and had felt every one of his deep shudders of pleasure reverberating through her flesh.

She hoped it had been much more than just a physical release for him. She knew it had been a while since he'd been intimate with anyone but, even so, it had felt like he had truly cared about her. He had made sure she'd been comfortable and at ease with him and had made sure she'd experienced pleasure before he'd taken his own. He'd coached her without coercing her to do bolder things. Had been passionate and yet achingly tender with her. How would she be able to pretend he was just her boss at work? Wouldn't everyone guess as soon as they saw her?

When she got to work Kate Harrison and Megan Brent were in the change room, putting their things in the lockers. 'Looks like the boss has got himself a new girlfriend,' Kate said as she hung up her coat and scarf.

Molly kept her gaze averted as she unlocked a locker. Was it somehow written on her face? Had she given off some clue? Could people actually tell she had spent the night in Lucas's arms? 'What makes you say that?' she asked.

'He actually smiled at us as he walked past,' Kate

said. 'Can you believe that? He never smiles. We reckon he got laid last night. Don't we, Megan?'

'Sure of it,' Megan said. 'I wonder who it is?'

Molly stashed her things inside the locker. She could see her cheeks were rosy red in the reflection in the little mirror hanging on the inside of the door. How soon before they put two and two together? Everyone knew she was sharing his house. It wasn't much of a step to sharing his bed as well, or so most people would assume.

How would Lucas deal with everyone talking about them? How would *she* deal with it? She didn't want anything to spoil her relationship with him. It was all too new and precious to her. She wanted time to feel her way with him, to help him see how wonderful being together could be. If a gossip-fest started he might bring things to an abrupt end. He put work before relationships and if their relationship threatened to jeopardise his career, she knew which he would choose.

'I don't think it'd be anyone from the hospital,' Kate said. 'He has a bit of a thing about staff hooking up with each other. He told off one of the residents for getting it on with a nurse in one of the storage rooms. We all thought he was going to have him fired.'

'Do you know who it is?' Megan asked Molly.

'Um...' Molly felt flustered. Should she say something? Oh, why hadn't they talked about this earlier? What was she supposed to do? Deny it? Broadcast it? Lie about it?

'You're renting a room at his place,' Kate said. 'Surely you'd be the first to know if he brought someone home. Who is it? Did you get a good look at her? What's she like?'

Molly turned to close her locker door before she faced the two women again. 'I don't think Dr Banning would appreciate me discussing his private life,' she said. 'I know I wouldn't appreciate him discussing mine.'

Kate lifted her brows as she exchanged a look with Megan. 'Right,' she said. 'Fair enough.'

Molly slipped her lanyard over her neck. 'I'd better get going,' she said, and hurriedly left.

Lucas headed back to ICU after speaking to the infectious diseases doctor about Tim Merrick's antibiotic cover. He hadn't seen Molly since he had left her in the shower that morning. He had intended to talk to her about how they were going to handle their relationship at work but he'd got a call about Tim's rising temperature and had had to rush to the hospital.

He wondered if she would feel uncomfortable about separating their private lives from their work ones. He was good at switching off his emotions but he had a feeling she might not find it as easy. She was the type to wear her heart on her sleeve. She was open and honest to a fault. He, on the other hand, preferred to play his cards close to his chest. He didn't want to be the subject of gossip and loathed people speculating about his private life. The thought of everyone picking apart his relationship with Molly was anathema to him. He didn't want to be ribbed about his involvement with her. He didn't want to be the butt of jokes or on the receiving end of teasing comments.

He wondered how long it would be before the news was out. It was more or less common knowledge that she was rooming at his place. How soon before people assumed they were sleeping together?

Being involved with Molly was an emotional minefield. She was only here for a short time. He wasn't sure how he was going to navigate the next few weeks. A short-term affair sounded good in theory, but how would it play out in practice? What if he didn't want her to leave when her time was up? What if she didn't want to go? His mind swirled with a torrent of thoughts. How would she face her parents if she chose to be with him? How would he face his? Their relationship would cause even more heartache. How could it not?

He was the last person her parents would want her to be with. He had torn apart their family. He couldn't undo the damage of that one moment in time. There was no way he could atone for the death of Matt. He had given years of his life to serving others, to saving others, but it still didn't make an iota of difference.

He could not bring Matt back.

Even if by some miracle her parents and his were OK about him being with Molly, there were still his own doubts over whether he could make her or anyone happy. He had spent so long on his own he wasn't sure he could handle the emotional intimacy of a long-term relationship. He had never been half of a couple before. His relationships—hook-ups was probably a more accurate term—had never involved the sharing of feelings, hopes, dreams, values and goals. He didn't know how to be emotionally available to a partner. He didn't know how to be emotionally available to *anyone.*

He kept that part of himself tightly locked down. His parents and brothers had all but given up on trying to draw him out. He didn't want anyone to see the bottomless black hole of despair deep inside him. He had concreted it over with work and responsibilities that would have burnt out a weaker man. He knew it wasn't healthy, he knew it wasn't going to make him happy either, but he had long ago resigned himself to a life lived without the contentment and fulfilment other people took for granted.

His hope was that Molly would finally come to see he was not worth the effort.

Molly was at Claire Mitchell's bedside as Lucas came into ICU. She had worked tirelessly with Claire each day and he had been impressed by her dedication and patience. Claire had a long road ahead of her and would have to spend months in a rehab facility, learning to walk and talk again. But at least she was going to make it. Her parents would still have their daughter, even if she wasn't quite as physically able as she had been.

Tim Merrick, on the other hand, was an ongoing nightmare. The CSF leak from his ear had increased overnight. The base-of-skull fracture had entered the middle-ear cavity and opened up a potential entry point of bacteria. Lucas had repeated an EEG but there was still little brain activity. The transplant team had contacted him earlier that morning but he had refused to enter into a discussion about harvesting Tim's organs. He was treating Tim hour by hour, refusing to give up hope, even though a part of him was seriously starting to doubt there would be any chance of him recovering. He kept thinking of Hamish Fisher, how shattered he had looked that morning as he had been discharged from hospital. Lucas remembered it all too well—the day he had walked out of the hospital, with his best mate lying cold and lifeless in the morgue.

At least Tim was still alive—for now.

'Claire, can you hear me?' Molly was saying. 'Open your eyes. Lift your arm. Wriggle your toes.'

'Is she responding?' Lucas asked.

'Yes, she opened her eyes a couple of times,' she said. 'She's fighting the ventilator. Her intracranial pressure and all other obs are stable. I think it's time to start weaning her off the ventilator and sedation. I've asked the nurse to let me know if her stats drop. How is Tim Merrick doing? I heard things got worse overnight.'

He gave her a grim look. 'I've started high-dose imipenem and gentamicin and I've just spoken to the ID doctor about recommendations for antibiotic cover. If we don't get on top of this quickly, his chance of a recovery is going to disappear. The next forty-eight hours are going to be critical.'

'Jacqui told me the transplant team called,' Molly said, giving him a pained look.

Lucas drew in a tight breath. 'Yes, but I'm not going to make any decision until we repeat the EEG a couple of times at least.'

'His parents seem resigned—'

'His parents are shocked and upset,' he said. 'They need more time to come to terms with their son's injuries. It's too early to say how things will pan out. Trust me, Molly. I know what I'm doing.'

She caught her lower lip with her teeth. 'I was wondering if you had a minute to talk…in private, I mean.'

'I'll be in my offIce in about twenty minutes,' he said. 'I have a couple more charts to write up first.'

Molly knocked on Lucas's open office door but he was on the phone and gestured to her to come in and sit down. She closed the door and came over to the chair opposite his desk, not sitting down but waiting for him to finish his call.

'Sorry about that,' he said, and placed his phone on the desk. 'It's been one of those mornings. Everyone wants everything yesterday.'

'Yes…'

He studied her for a moment. 'Are you OK?' he asked.

Molly let out a little breath. 'I was wondering how we're going to handle this…um, situation between us. A couple of the nurses were talking in the change room when I came in this morning. I didn't know what to say.'

'There's nothing *to* say,' he said.

'It's not that simple,' she said. 'I think people are going to put two and two together pretty quickly. I'm not sure how to deal with it. We didn't get a chance to talk about it this morning.'

He blew out an impatient breath. 'Personally I can't see why it's anyone's business. I don't go around asking staff members who they're sleeping with, do you?'

'No, of course not.'

He raked a hand through his hair as he leaned back forcefully in his chair. 'What do they want us to do? Release a press statement or something? *God*. Why don't these people have lives of their own instead of speculating about everyone else's?'

'If you'd rather not have people know about us then I'll deny any rumours.'

He leaned forward again and dropped his hand back down on the desk with a little thump. 'These things have a habit of fizzling out after a week or two,' he said. 'It's best just to ignore the speculation.'

'I'm sorry…'

He gave her a wry look. 'Why are *you* apologising?'

Molly dropped her shoulders. 'I seem to have made your life even more complicated.'

'Yes, well, it's not as if it's going to be that way for ever,' he said, making a business of shuffling the papers on his desk.

'You can come right out and say it, you know,' she said, hurt at how he seemed to have filed her away too, as if she was something temporary he had to deal with. 'You don't have to spare my feelings or anything. I understand this is just a fling between us.'

His expression tightened as his gaze met hers. 'The one thing you can't accuse me of is not being honest with you,' he said. 'This is all I can give you.'

'Fine,' Molly said in a perverse attempt to act all modern and casual about it. 'We'll have our fling and once it's time for me to leave, I'll just kiss you goodbye and get on with my life and you'll get on with yours. Does that sound like a plan?'

His jaw worked for a moment. 'As long as we both know where we stand.'

'But of course,' she said. 'If anyone asks, I'll just say we're housemates with benefits. How does that sound?'

His forehead was deeply grooved with a brooding

frown. 'Couldn't you think of a better way to put it than that?' he asked.

'Get with the times, Lucas,' Molly said as she gave him a cheery fingertip wave from the door.

Lucas came back from helping the registrars with a new patient when Jacqui pulled him to one side. 'What's going on between you and Molly Drummond?' she asked.

Here we go, he thought with a roll of his eyes. This would be the first of no doubt many comments he was going to get. 'Why do you ask?' he said.

'Everyone's saying you're a couple now,' she said, her eyes bright with interest. 'Is it true? Are you officially together?'

Lucas was still trying to get his head around Molly's term for their relationship. Call him old-fashioned, but he didn't like the sound of housemates with benefits. It sounded like he was taking advantage of her. He hadn't invited her to stay in his house so he could sleep with her. That had just…happened. OK, well, sure, he'd *wanted* it to happen. He *still* wanted it to happen, but it couldn't happen for ever.

He wasn't a for ever type of guy.

'You know I never discuss my private life at work,' he said as he continued briskly on his way.

Jacqui kept pace with him like a little Chihuahua snapping at his heels. 'Come on, Lucas,' she said. 'What would it hurt to get it out in the open? She's such a sweetheart and it's so cool that you've known each other for years and years. I bet your parents and hers will be thrilled to bits. It's so romantic.'

He threw her a hard look. 'Don't you have work to do?'

'You make such a lovely couple,' she said. 'I bet you'll make gorgeous babies together. Will you invite me to the wedding? I've always wanted to go to Australia. That's where you'll have it, won't you?'

Lucas dismissed her with a look. 'There's not going to be a wedding,' he said, pushing open his office door. 'Excuse me. Some of us around here have work to do.'

Molly was home first and spent some time playing with Mittens before she started cooking dinner. She wondered if she was doing the right thing in setting candles and flowers on the table, but she just couldn't get her head around being *that* casual about things. Somehow waiting naked in bed for him wasn't quite her. She wanted to read his mood first, see what sort of day he'd had. Help him relax and put work stresses aside. She wanted to show she cared about him as a person, not just as someone she was having a fling with. She put on some romantic music on the sophisticated sound system that was wired through the house and opened a bottle of wine she had bought on the way home.

Glancing at her watch a couple of times, she wondered when Lucas would be home. She hadn't seen him since their conversation in his office. She had been busy with a new admission and he had been called to a meeting with the family of an elderly patient who wasn't expected to make it through the night.

He came in just after nine p.m. Molly got off the sofa in the sitting room where she had been whiling away the time with a glass of wine and met him in the foyer. 'Hard day?' she asked when she saw his heavy frown.

'You could say that,' he said, shrugging off his coat.

'I made dinner for you,' she said.

His frown deepened as he hung up his coat. 'You shouldn't have bothered.'

'It was no bother,' Molly said. 'I love cooking. I set up the dining room. It looks fabulous.'

He turned from the coat stand, his frown even darker on his brow. 'What for?' he asked.

'Because it's a beautiful room that's just crying out to be used,' she said. 'What's your problem? You won't eat out. I thought this would be the next best thing. Kind of like a date at home.'

He moved past her on his way to the stairs. 'I'm not hungry.'

Molly felt her spirits plummet. 'What's wrong?' she asked. 'Have I upset you?'

His hands gripped the balustrade so tightly his knuckles whitened beneath the skin. 'Why would you think that?' he asked.

She folded her lips together, feeling horribly uncertain and unsophisticated. 'I was so looking forward to you coming home,' she said. 'I thought you would be looking forward to it, too. I guess I was wrong. You'd obviously rather be alone.' She swung away to the kitchen, determined not to cry.

'Molly.'

'It's all right, I quite understand,' she said, turning back to face him. 'We obviously have different expectations about how this is going to work. I'm afraid I haven't read the latest edition of the *Having A Fling* handbook. Maybe you could give me a few tips. Clearly soft music and candles are out. Perhaps I should've just draped myself over your bed instead.'

He shoved a hand through his hair and blew out a weary sigh. 'I'm sorry,' he said. 'I'm in a rotten mood. It's wrong to take it out on you. Forgive me?'

Molly gave him a huffy look.

'Come here,' he commanded gently but firmly.

She angled her body slightly away from him, her chin up and her arms across her middle. 'I'm not that much of a pushover, you know.'

He moved to where she was standing and gently un-peeled her arms from around her body and gathered her close against him. 'I'm sorry for being a such a bear,' he said. 'I've got a lot on my mind just now. I'm used to coming home and being alone with my thoughts.'

Molly looked up at him with a little pleat of worry on her brow. 'Do you want me to move out?'

He smoothed her frown away with the pad of his thumb. 'That's the very last thing I want you to do,' he said. 'The house feels different with you here. It's warmer, more like a home.'

'I should've checked with you first about dinner,' she said as she toyed with one of the buttons on his shirt. 'I didn't think…I'm sorry.'

'It's fine, Molly,' he said. 'Really.'

'I know it's been awkward for you today with every-one talking about us…'

'They'll stop in a day or two when they realise it's business as usual,' he said. 'I'm usually pretty good at ignoring that sort of thing.'

Molly looked up at him again. 'Are you really not hungry?' she asked.

His eyes smouldered as they held hers. 'My appetite is being stimulated as we speak.'

'I hope I've prepared enough to satisfy you,' she said with a little smile.

He scooped her up in his arms. 'Let's go and find out, shall we?'

CHAPTER NINE

LUCAS WOKE FROM a deep sleep to answer what he thought was his phone. He reached across Molly, who was still soundly asleep, and picked up the phone from the bedside table. 'Lucas Banning,' he said.

There was a shocked gasp and then silence from the other end.

Molly shifted sleepily against him. 'Who is it?' she asked.

He handed her the phone. 'I think it's for you,' he said. 'I thought it was my phone. Sorry.'

She sat up and pushed the tousled hair out of her eyes. 'Hello?'

Lucas heard Molly's mother on the other end. 'I think I called you at a bad time. Do you want me to call back when you're alone?'

Molly glanced at Lucas. 'No, it's fine, Mum... Um, how are you?'

Lucas got off the bed and went to the bathroom to give her some privacy. When he came out again she had hung up was sitting on the edge of the bed with a strained look on her face. 'That was my mother,' she said.

'So I gathered.'

'She was a bit shocked that you answered my phone.'

'I gathered that, too,' he said.

She nibbled at her bottom lip for a moment. 'It's not that she doesn't approve of me getting involved with you…'

'You don't have to pull your punches, Molly,' he said. 'I realise I'm not her top pick as a partner for you.'

'She'll be fine about it once she gets her head around it,' she said. 'It was a shock to find out like that, that's all. I should've called her and told her.'

'I guess it'll be your father calling you next to tear strips off you,' Lucas said, snatching up his trousers and shaking out the creases before he put them on.

She got off the bed and came over and put her arms around his waist. 'I can handle my father,' she said. '*We* are the only people in this relationship. It's got nothing to do with anyone else. Not at work or back at home in Australia. This is about us, here and now.'

Lucas let out a long exhalation and gathered her close. The here and the now wasn't his greatest worry. It was what happened next that had him lying awake at night. Within a few weeks she would be heading home. He couldn't ask her to stay with him, to give up her life back home, all her friends and family, all that was familiar and dear to her. How could he ask it of her? He could more or less cope with the parental opposition but he couldn't cope with hurting her by not being good enough for her. How could he ever be good enough when he had caused her more hurt than anyone?

He kissed the top of her head and put her from him. 'I have to get moving,' he said. 'I have a couple of meetings this morning and another one after work. I'm not sure what time I'll be home.'

'I thought I'd touch base with Emma Wingfield about the fundraising dinner,' she said. 'Would you be agreeable to having it here? It would cut down the costs of hiring a venue. I understand if you don't want to. I know it's a lot to ask.'

Lucas saw the little spark of enthusiasm in her eyes. What would it hurt to let her go to town with the dinner? It would be something to look back on once she had gone. 'Sure,' he said. 'Why not? Let me know what you need. I'll get Gina to give you a hand.'

She stood up on tiptoe and kissed him on the lips. 'Thank you,' she said. 'I'll make sure it's a night to remember.'

Molly hadn't long got home from work that evening when her father called.

'What the hell do you think you're doing?' he said without preamble.

'Hi, Dad,' she said. 'I'm fine, and you?'

'Of all the people in London you could hook up with,' he went on, 'why him? I had to drag it out of your mother. She wasn't going to tell me but I knew something was up as soon as I spoke to her. When were you going to tell me you're sleeping with the enemy?'

Molly rolled her eyes. 'I'm not going to discuss my love life with you, Dad. Lucas and I are seeing each other and that's all I'm prepared to say.'

'He'll break your heart,' he said. 'You just see. It's what he does best. He'll use you and then walk away. He just wants his conscience eased. I reckon he thinks a little fling with you will fool everyone into thinking we've all moved on. But I'll never forgive him. Do you hear me? I will not allow that man to come within a bull's roar of me or any of my family.'

'How is your new family?' Molly asked.

'Don't use that tone with me, young lady,' her father said. 'I'm telling you right now, if you continue to see him I will never speak to you again. Do you hear me? It's him or me. Make your choice.'

'Dad, you're being ridiculous,' she said. 'Isn't it time to move on? Matt would be appalled by your attitude. You know he would.'

'I mean it, Molly. I'll disown you. You see if I won't.'

Molly fought to contain her temper. There was so much she wanted to throw at her father. All the times he had let her and her mother down. All the times he had criticised her for not being as good as Matt at things. All the times she had felt unloved and undervalued by him. It bubbled up inside her like a cauldron of caustic soda. 'You know, that's exactly the sort of thing I've come to expect from you,' she said. 'When things don't go your way, you have a tantrum or throw in the towel, just like you did with Mum. I'm not giving up Lucas just to appease you. If you want to disown me then go right ahead. It's your choice.'

'You're the one making the choice,' her father said. 'Once I hang up this phone, that's it. I won't be calling again, not unless I hear you've ended things with Lucas Banning.'

The line went dead.

Molly pressed the off button on her phone just as the front door opened and Lucas stepped in.

His brows moved together. 'Your father?'

'Yes,' she said with a little slump of her shoulders.

He came over and put a gentle hand on the nape of her neck. 'Hey.'

Molly looked up at him through moist eyes. 'I've never been able to please him,' she said. 'It wouldn't matter who I was seeing, he wouldn't approve. He doesn't love me, not like a father should love his daughter. If he loved me he'd be happy for me.'

He drew her close against his chest, his hand rhythmically stroking her head where it rested against him. 'He does love you, Molly,' he said. 'He's just afraid to lose you. It colours everything he does. I would be the same in his place.'

She gave a heavy sigh and began to fiddle with his loosened tie with her fingers. 'I thought you weren't coming home early,' she said.

'We got through the agenda of the meeting in record time,' he said. 'I thought we could go out to dinner.'

She blinked at him in surprise. 'Dinner? As in out somewhere? In a restaurant? In public?'

He gave her a rueful half-smile. 'I really am dreadfully out of practice, aren't I?' he said. 'Yes, out in public in a fancy restaurant.'

Molly smiled as she flung her arms around his neck. 'I would love to.'

Lucas was putting on his jacket at the foot of the staircase when Molly came down half an hour later. Her perfume preceded her—a fresh, flowery fragrance with a hint of something exotic underneath. He turned to look at her, his mouth almost dropping open when he took in her appearance. She was classy and sexy, modern and yet conservative, sweet and sultry. Her mid-thigh-length black velvet dress clung to her figure like a glove. Her high heels showcased her racehorse-slim ankles and calves, and she had styled her hair in a teased messy ponytail at the back of her head, giving her a wild-child look. Her lips were shiny with lip gloss, her eyes smoky with eye shadow and eyeliner.

It was a knockout combination and he wondered how she had managed to get to the age of twenty-seven without some guy snapping her up and carting her off to be his wife and the mother of his children.

He tried to ignore the pang he felt at the thought of her ripe with someone else's child. He didn't want to think about another man taking her in his arms and making love to her. He didn't want to imagine another man's mouth pressed against those soft, sweet lips.

He wanted her to himself, but how could he have her with the past like a stain lying between them? It would always be there. It would seep into and discolour every aspect of their lives. If they married and had children, he would one day have to explain to them what had happened to their uncle. How would any child look at its father knowing he was responsible for the death of another human being? There had been a time when he had envisaged himself with a family similar to the one he had grown up in. He'd had great role models in his parents. They were strict but fair, loving and supportive, committed to their children and to each other. He had seen them weather some of life's toughest dramas and yet they had never faltered in their devotion to each other and their boys. He had assumed he would have a similar relationship but, of course, that's not how things had panned out.

It was different now.

It had to be.

'You look beautiful,' Lucas said.

Her eyes shone as they met his. 'You look pretty hot yourself.'

He tucked her arm underneath his. 'Shall we go?'

The restaurant Lucas had booked was a fifteen-minute drive from his house. He barely spoke on the journey, other than to point out places of interest like a jaded tour guide.

Molly glanced at him surreptitiously from time to time, but each time she looked at him his brow was lined with a frown as if he was chewing over something mentally taxing. Was he regretting issuing his invitation to have dinner? All her insecurities came out to play. Maybe he was having second thoughts about their involvement.

After all, she had been the one who had made the first move when she had found him sleeping in the library the other night. If it hadn't been for her bending down to kiss him they might not have become involved at all. They might still be just housemates, two ships passing in the night as they went about their busy working lives. Did he regret their involvement? Did he want to put a time limit on it?

What was going to happen when it was time for her to leave? Would he sever the connection or expect her to? They had by tacit agreement avoided mentioning the future. But it was still something that lurked in the background. Molly could even sense the ticking clock on their relationship. She had been here almost three weeks. That left only nine to go. Each day was another day closer to the time she would be leaving. Would he ask her to stay? Or would he be relieved when she got on that plane back to Australia?

'Are you OK?' Molly asked after a long stretch of silence.

He glanced at her distractedly. 'Pardon?'

'You seem a bit preoccupied. You've hardly said a word since you pointed out the Houses of Parliament.'

He reached out and took her hand and brought it up to his mouth and kissed it. 'Sorry,' he said. 'I have a lot on my mind just now. Work stuff. Brian Yates had got a bit behind with some paperwork. It's a nightmare sorting it all out.'

'When was the last time you took a holiday?' she asked.

'I went to a conference in Manchester three months ago.'

She looked at him askance. 'The one where you had the one-night stand?'

His expression tightened. 'Yes.'

'That's hardly what I'd call a holiday,' Molly said. 'I meant a proper holiday. Lying on the beach somewhere, drinking cocktails. That sort of thing.'

He lifted one shoulder. 'I'm not big on cocktails. And I've seen enough people dying with melanomas to put me off lying in the sun for life.'

'All the same, you can't expect to work all the time without a break,' she said. 'It's not good for your health.

People in their early thirties can still get heart attacks, you know.'

'I know,' he said. 'That's why I go to the gym. I go to a twenty-four-hour one a couple of blocks from home. I have a couple of guest passes if you want to try it out some time.'

'I'm not much of a gym bunny,' Molly confessed. 'I prefer long walks in the fresh air.'

'Fair enough,' he said.

Lucas parked the car and came around to open her door. Molly loved it that he had those old-fashioned good manners. He had been brought up to treat women with respect and consideration. She felt feminine and protected as he helped her out of the car with a light hand at her elbow.

Once inside the restaurant they were shown to a cosy table in a candlelit corner. Soft ambient music was playing, making the atmosphere romantic and intimate. 'Have you been here before?' she asked once the waiter had left them to study the menu.

'Not for a long time,' Lucas said. 'I think it's changed hands a couple of times since then but it got a good write-up recently.'

The waiter took their order and left them with their drinks. Molly was conscious of the silence stretching between them. 'I had the meeting with Emma today,' she said. 'She was really excited about the dinner dance at your house. We've marked a tentative date for the first Saturday in May. We're thinking about fifty or sixty couples. The more exclusive it is the better. People don't mind paying top dollar for something that's really special.'

'Sounds like a good plan.'

'And we also thought we might have a theme,' she said.

He gave her a forbidding look. 'Don't ask me to dress up in a ridiculous costume.'

Molly gave him a teasing smile. 'Where's your sense of fun?' she asked. 'I think you'd look fabulous in a Superman costume.'

'No way,' he said, glowering at her. 'Don't even think about it. It's not going to happen.'

'It's all right,' she said, still smiling at him. 'We thought we'd have a black and white theme. Everyone has to wear either black or white or both. We'll decorate the ballroom the same. It'll be very glam.'

'I think I can manage to rustle up a tuxedo,' he said. 'But I should warn you I'm not much of a dancer. I have two left feet.'

'I can help you with that,' she said. 'Mum sent me to debutante school. It won't take me long to teach you to burn up the dance floor.'

He gave a noncommittal grunt as the waiter came over with their meals.

It was raining when they came out of the restaurant. Lucas took off his jacket and used it like an umbrella over Molly. 'Aren't you freezing?' she asked as they made a dash for the car.

'I'm used to it,' he said. 'Mind your step. The pavement's uneven in places.'

It was a quiet drive home but Molly thought Lucas had lost some of his earlier tension. He had started to relax a little after the entrée and had even smiled at one of her work anecdotes. For a while she had felt like they were any other couple having a meal out together. But every now and again she would look across at him and find him with a frown between his eyes.

'I enjoyed tonight,' she said as they walked into the house a short time later.

'I did too,' he said.

'Our first date.'

'Pardon?'

Molly looked at him. 'That was our first proper date.'

'So how did it measure up?' he asked.

'I don't know,' she said. 'It's not over yet.'

A half-smile lurked around the edges of his mouth. 'You seem pretty sure about that.'

She stepped up to him and placed her arms around his neck. 'I want to dance with you.'

'Right now?'

She pushed his thigh back with one of hers. 'Right now.'

A gleam came into his eyes as he started to move with her along the floor. 'I think I could get used to this dancing thing,' he said. 'How am I doing?'

She smiled as he brought her up close to his aroused body. 'You're a natural. You have all the right moves.'

He stopped dancing, his eyes burning as they held hers. 'I want to make love with you. Now.'

Molly shivered as he gripped her hips and held her harder against him. 'Right now?' she asked.

'Right now.'

He swooped down and captured her mouth beneath his in a sizzling hot kiss, his tongue driving through to find hers in a sexy lust-driven tango. Molly felt her senses careen out of control as his aroused body probed the softness of hers. Desire was hot and wet between her thighs as he moved her backwards along the foyer in a blind dance of passion until her back was against the wall.

Her hands went to his shirt, tugging and pulling until it was out of his trousers and unbuttoned. She slid her hands all over his chest, caressing, stroking until she came to the fastener on his waistband. She worked on it blindly as his mouth masterfully commandeered hers. Electricity pulsed like a powerful current through her body as his hands shaped her breasts through her clothes. Her nipples felt achingly tight, her breasts full and sensitive.

Her insides quivered as he deepened his kiss, his tongue stabbing and stroking, thrusting and gliding until she was mindless with need. She could feel it building in her body. All the sensitive nerves stretching and straining to reach the pinnacle of pleasure she craved. It was centred low and deep in her body, the feminine core of her alive and aching for the intimate invasion of his body.

Finally she freed him from his trousers. He was thick and full and like satin wrapped steel in her fingers. She caressed him with increasing pressure and speed, delighting in the low deep grunts of approval he was giving. Spurred on by his reaction, she dropped to her knees in front of him and brought him to her mouth.

He gripped the sides of her head. 'No, you don't have to do that,' he said.

'I want to do it,' Molly said. 'I want to taste you like you tasted me.'

He gave a muttered curse as she closed her lips over him. She felt him shudder against the walls of her mouth as he fought to control his response. It thrilled her to have such feminine power over him. He was so thick and so strong and yet he was at the mercy of her touch.

After a few moments he pulled out with a gasping groan. 'No more.' He hauled her to her feet and roughly pulled up her dress until it was bunched around her waist.

She clung to him with one hand as the other peeled away her tights and knickers. Excitement raced along the network of her veins like rocket fuel. She was breathless with it, impatient with it, hungry for every deliciously erotic thing he had in store.

He positioned her against the wall and thrust into her with a deep primal groan that lifted every hair on her head. Her sensitised flesh gripped him tightly, drawing him in, holding him, squeezing him, tormenting him. He rocked against her almost savagely. She held onto his hips, with him all the way, wanting more speed, more pressure, more of that tantalising friction. She was getting closer and closer to the point of no return. She could feel every nerve preparing itself for the free-fall into paradise.

And then she was there, falling, spinning, falling, spinning, delicious contraction after delicious contraction moving like an earthquake through her flesh. She gasped and cried as her body shook and shuddered against his, her hands digging into his taut buttocks as he finally emptied himself.

Molly held him tightly against her as her breathing calmed. She could feel the stickiness of his essence between her legs. It was so incredibly intimate to be that close to him. She had never felt so close to someone.

It was not just the physical experience. There was something much deeper and elemental in how she responded to him and he to her. It was like they were meant to be together—two halves that made a complete whole. She felt a connection with him that went beyond their similar upbringings. It was as if he was the only person who could love her the way she wanted and needed to be loved—with his whole being, his body, his mind and his soul. What woman didn't want a love like that?

Molly knew he was capable of that sort of love. What she didn't know was if he would allow himself to be free of the past in order to act on it.

Lucas brushed her hair away from her face, his eyes dark and serious now the passion had abated. 'I wasn't too rough with you, was I?' he asked.

Molly was touched that he was concerned. 'You were amazing,' she said, looking up at him. '*We* are amazing together. I never thought it could be this good. It keeps getting better and better.'

He tucked some of her hair behind one of her ears, his gaze becoming shadowed, his expression twisted with ruefulness. 'We are amazing together...'

'But,' she said. 'That's what you were going to say, wasn't it? There's always a but with you, isn't there?'

A mask slipped over his features. He drew in a breath and slowly released it. 'Molly...'

'There doesn't have to be a but,' Molly said. 'We can be amazing together for always. You know we can.'

He put his hands on her wrists and unlocked her

hold from around his neck. 'We've already talked about this,' he said. 'I told you what I can give you. There's no point going over it all the time in the hope that I'll somehow change my mind. This is the way it is. You have to accept it.'

Molly blinked back burning tears, her chest feeling as if hard fists were pummelling against her heart. 'Are you really going to just end our relationship when it's time for me to leave?' she asked. 'Have you already circled the calendar or marked it your diary? Have you've written, *"Finish things with Molly"*?'

His features were pulled tight. 'Think about it, Molly,' he said. 'You'd gain me but you'd lose your family. Your father will cut you off. He's probably already threatened to do so. Yes, I thought so. Your mother will make an effort but every time she sees me she'll think of the son she lost. And then, if we were ever to have children...' His throat rose and fell and his voice came out hoarse as he continued, 'What will you tell them when they ask about their uncle? Will you tell them their father *killed* him?'

Molly swallowed the knot of anguish clogging her throat. How could she get him to change his mind? Could they have a chance in spite of everything that had happened? Surely other people overcame tragic circumstances. Why couldn't they? Was it because he didn't love her? He hadn't said anything, but, then, neither had she. He didn't seem the type to be saying 'I love you' at the drop of a hat. But, then, she had never told anyone other than her parents that she loved them. But she sensed that Lucas cared very deeply for her. He showed it in so many little ways.

Was that why he refused to promise her a future? He wanted her to be free to move on from the tragedy of the past and he believed she couldn't do that if she was with him. He was determined their relationship had a strict time limit.

Molly suddenly realised what it must be like for couples during times of war and separation. Of having to live in the moment, of not being sure of what the future would hold, clinging to one another, grateful for every tiny chance to be together. Not making plans but living and loving while they could. It was the same for long-term married couples or even younger couples where one partner was facing the imminent death of the other due to a terminal illness. She had seen them time and time again in ICU. The clock ticking down, each moment more and more precious as it could very well be the last.

How did people do it? How would *she* do it? She wanted fifty, sixty, seventy years—a lifetime to love Lucas, not just a matter of weeks.

Molly couldn't think of a time when she hadn't loved him. When she had been a little kid she had loved him, but that had been more of a hero-worship thing. He had been her older brother's best friend, someone she'd admired from afar. He had always treated her well. He had been far kinder to her than her own brother. Growing up without sisters had made him particularly mindful of the feelings and sensibilities of little girls. He had always treated her with respect and, to some degree, affectionate indulgence. How could she not fall in love with him as an adult? He was the same kind, gentle man—a man who gave up so much of his life for others. Matt's death hadn't caused that other focused part of his personality, rather it had just enhanced it.

But loving Lucas came with a hefty price tag. Her father had already made it clear that he wanted nothing more to do with her if she continued to be involved with Lucas. After the initial shock her mother seemed more accepting, but how long before she too worried that Molly was being short-changed emotionally? No mother wanted to see her daughter with a man who wasn't capable of loving her.

And then there was the issue of children. She wanted a family. She had wanted to be a mother since she had been a little kid. She had nursed every baby animal she had been able to get her hands on, adopting every stray she could in her effort to nurture them.

Lucas was the only man she could imagine as the father of her children. She wanted to feel his baby moving inside her womb. She wanted to feel the march of the contractions through her abdomen that would bring their baby into the world and she wanted to see his face as she gave birth. She wanted to see him hold their baby in his strong arms, to cradle it against his broad chest, to protect and love it as tenderly as he had been loved and nurtured.

But now all those hopes and dreams she had stored in her heart for all this time would never be realised. It was so bitter-sweet to know he loved her but was prepared to give her up because he felt that was best for her.

He was wrong.

He *had* to be wrong.

She would be miserable without him. She would be heartbroken without him in her life. She would be totally devastated to have loved and lost him. She wanted him to live life with her, to share the highs and lows and all the little bits in between: the happy bits; the sad bits; the angry bits; and the funny bits—all the things that enriched a couple's life together.

Surely he would see that eventually? It might take more than the nine weeks left, but surely he would come to realise that it was better to be together than apart? How could she *make* him see it? Would she have to take a gamble on it? To spend the next few weeks in the hope that he would not be able let her go at the end?

Molly looked up at him through misty eyes. 'Can we not talk about this any more?' she said. 'I just want to pretend we are just like any other couple in a new relationship. Can we do that, please?'

He brushed her quivering bottom lip with the pad of his thumb. 'Of course,' he said, and bending his head he softly covered her mouth with his.

CHAPTER TEN

MOLLY WAS AT work a few days later, supervising Claire Mitchell's transfer to the rehabilitation unit. Claire was not fully mobile but she was completely conscious and responding to commands. Her tracheotomy tube had been removed and the hole taped closed, but it would take up to two weeks for the wound to heal over completely. Claire could speak in a whisper but her words were still slurred and a little jumbled and she still had some short-term memory problems. Her parents were relieved but clearly a little daunted at the long road ahead for their only child.

Claire would probably spend months in the rehab centre and was unlikely to regain the full use of her legs. It was a heartbreaking thought that a young woman who had been so fit and athletic, who before the accident had been at the top of her game in equestrian events, was now no longer able to take even a few paces, let alone vault up into a saddle and ride her beloved horse.

Jacqui walked back with Molly to the ICU office once the orderly had left with Claire and her parents. 'For a while there I thought that poor girl wasn't going to make it at all,' she said. 'You should have seen her when she first came in. A bit like our Tim, poor chap.

You just never know how they're going to end up, do you?'

'No, you don't.' Molly glanced to where Tim's parents were by his bedside in ICU, keeping their lonely vigil. They came in each day, spending hours in his cubicle, talking to him, playing his favourite music on an MP3 player, stroking him and praying over him with the hospital chaplain.

Lucas was still treating him hour by hour, stubbornly refusing to give up hope of a recovery. The CSF leak had stopped once they'd got control of the infection, and while a subsequent scan had shown a little brain activity, it was still not as positive as everyone had hoped.

Hamish Fisher had been in just about every day. Molly had watched on one of his first visits as Lucas had taken him aside and talked to him in his quiet, supportive way. It had been particularly moving to see Tim's parents hug Hamish by their son's bedside. There were lots of tears but no harsh words or accusations—so different from her father, who after all this time was still so antagonistic towards Lucas.

'Lucas still thinks there's a chance with Tim Merrick,' Jacqui said, following the line of Molly's gaze. 'He's getting a bit of flak from some of his colleagues, though.'

'Yes, I know,' Molly said, thinking of some of the angry exchanges she'd either witnessed or heard when Lucas had been on the phone. Lucas had given Tim mannitol a couple of times to reduce brain swelling and he had stopped the steroids. This was considered controversial by some as high-dose steroids were commonly used to reduce brain swelling, with mannitol generally only used in the acute situation, straight after the occurrence of an injury. But Lucas was concerned the steroids might suppress Tim's resistance to infection so he had stopped them and closely monitored intracranial pressure.

'So how are things going between you two?' Jacqui asked with a twinkling look. 'Lucas won't tell me a thing, damn him.'

'Things are fine,' Molly answered evasively. She didn't want to talk about her relationship with Lucas. It was precious and private. Their workplace relationship was friendly but professional. She was careful not to overstep the mark in any way. But there were times when she caught his eye and a secret message would pass between them. She would hum with longing all day until she got home. Sometimes she would barely get in the door before he reached for her. Other times he took his time, torturing her with long drawn-out foreplay that had her begging for mercy.

But not a day went past when she didn't long that they were indeed like any other young couple starting out together, without the past casting its dark shadow over them. Over the last few days she had found herself thinking wistfully of an engagement ring and a wedding gown. She had even wandered past a high street wedding designer on one of her walks. She had stood for long minutes in the freezing cold, wishing she was like the young bride in there with her mother, excitedly trying on gowns. She had turned away with a sinkhole of sadness inside her stomach. How would she ever be a bride if she couldn't be with Lucas? She didn't want anyone else. She couldn't think of being with anyone else. She was wired to love him and only him.

'Have you thought of staying on?' Jacqui asked. 'Your time with us is racing away. It'll be over before you know it.'

Tell me about it, Molly thought with a spasm of pain near her heart. 'I have a job lined up at home,' she said. 'It's at a big city teaching hospital close to where my mother lives. They held the post open for me while I came here. I'd feel bad if I didn't show up. Anyway, isn't the person I'm filling in for over here coming back from maternity leave?'

'Yes, but I thought Lucas, being director, might be able to wangle a position for you,' Jacqui said. 'It reeks of nepotism but who cares about that?'

'I don't think Lucas would do anything that wasn't fair and above board,' Molly said. 'Anyway, I wouldn't want him to.'

'You're good for him,' Jacqui said. 'He still works too damn hard but he seems a lot happier in himself since you've been here. I've been quite worried about him, to tell you the truth. I've never met a more driven doctor. I keep telling him he'll drive himself into an early grave if he doesn't let up a bit. He hasn't taken a holiday in I don't know how long.'

'I've been saying much the same thing,' Molly said.

'Maybe he'll take some time off and visit you back in the home country,' Jacqui said. 'Nothing like absence to make the heart grow fonder.'

Molly stretched her mouth in a brief pretence of a smile. 'Let's hope so.'

'You love him, don't you?' Jacqui's expression was full of mother-hen concern.

Molly sighed as she straightened some notes on the desk. 'I'll get over it.'

'Will you?'

Molly looked at the ward clerk's concerned expression. 'I'll have to, won't I?' she said. 'This is just for here and now.'

'But you want the whole package.' It was a statement, not a question. And it was the truth.

'Don't most women?' Molly asked.

'But he's not talking marriage and babies, is he?' Jacqui said. 'He told me point-blank there wasn't going to be a wedding when I asked him about it the other day. It doesn't make sense. Why wouldn't he want to marry you? He's old school right to his backbone. He's not one of these playboys who want their cake and eat it too. He doesn't say much, but anyone can see he's a family man at heart.'

Molly looked at the stack of papers on the desk again, absently flicking through the top right-hand corners of the pages with a fingertip. 'It's complicated...'

'It's because of your brother, isn't it?' Jacqui said. 'I've been watching him with Tim and that young friend of his Hamish, the one who was driving. That's why Lucas is so hell bent on keeping Tim alive. He was driving when your brother was killed, wasn't he?'

'It was an accident,' Molly said, looking at her again. 'It wasn't his fault. A kangaroo jumped out just as he came around the bend. There was nothing he could do. He didn't see it in time.'

'How sad,' Jacqui said. 'I've always wondered why

he's so hard on himself. He works harder than any other doctor I know. Poor Lucas. And poor you.'

'It was a long time ago,' Molly said. 'I'd prefer it if you kept this to yourself. We're all trying to move on from it.'

'But you haven't moved on from it, or at least Lucas hasn't,' Jacqui said. 'But, then, one doesn't move on from something like that. I guess you just have to learn to live with it.'

'I don't think Lucas sees it quite that way,' Molly said. 'He's punishing himself. He's been punishing himself for the last seventeen years. I hate seeing him do that to himself. Matt wouldn't have wanted him to do that to himself. It's all such a mess and there's nothing I can do to fix it.'

Jacqui gave Molly's arm a gentle squeeze. 'Your job is to love him, not to fix him,' she said. 'The rest is up to fate or destiny.'

If only fate and destiny weren't so damned capricious, Molly thought in despair as she walked back to ICU.

Lucas looked at the most recent scans of Tim Merrick's brain with Harry Clark, one of the more senior neurologists on staff.

'There's some activity but not much,' Harry said. 'I've seen a couple of cases where the patient has recovered after scans like this but it's not the norm.' He turned and looked at Lucas with a grim expression. 'He might not thank you for keeping him alive if he has to spend the rest of his days sitting slumped and drooling in a chair. Nor might his parents if it comes to that.'

Lucas tried to ignore the prickle of apprehension that had been curdling his stomach for days. Claire Mitchell had been moved to the rehab unit, which was a positive outcome considering how bleak things had looked when she had first been admitted. But she was going to have a very different life from the one she had known before. He had seen many patients and their families just like her struggle with what life had dished up.

But he didn't want to see Hamish Fisher go through the living hell he had gone through—*was still* going through. He wanted a miracle. He wanted it so badly, not just for Tim and his devoted parents. He wanted it for Hamish and he wanted it for himself. Tim might not have the life he'd had before, but he would still be alive. That was all that mattered.

'Wouldn't most parents want their kid to stay alive, no matter what?' Lucas asked.

Harry let out a long breath. 'Some do, some don't,' he said. 'I've had parents divided over a child's treatment. We had a case a few years back, a kid with severe epilepsy. He'd had one too many seizures and suffered oxygen deprivation. He was virtually vegetative. The father wanted to withdraw treatment. He was adamant about it. He didn't want to see his kid suffer any more. He'd spent fifteen years watching his boy suffer. The mother… Well, I guess that's what us men will never truly understand—the mother bond. She wanted her boy alive, no matter what state he was in.'

'What happened?'

'The parents divorced,' Harry said. 'The mother looked after that kid on her own for a couple of years and then one night he died in his sleep. I've often wondered if the father regretted not being there, helping her.'

'The kid could have lived for another twenty years,' Lucas pointed out.

'Yes,' Harry said with gravely. 'But would he have wanted to?'

Molly was late getting home after sending off the last of the invitations to the dinner dance. Everyone was getting excited about the event. It was the topic of every conversation at the hospital. The exclusivity element had created a furore, which she and Emma had milked for all it was worth. They had kept twenty-five double tickets back and had put them up for bidding on the hospital website.

The money they were raising was beyond anything they had imagined and it was thrilling to think people were so keen to be involved. Even the caterers had offered their services free of charge, and the string quartet—one of whom was a neurosurgical registrar at the hospital—had also offered to perform without charging a fee.

Molly couldn't wait to tell Lucas. She knew he would be pleased that so much money would be raised for the unit. Hospitals had to work so hard to meet their budgets and there was rarely money left over for any extras. With the money she and Emma were raising, new monitoring equipment could be purchased so patients like Emma would benefit in the future.

Mittens came over to Molly with a plaintive meow as soon as she walked through the front door. She bent down to stroke him and noticed he was wearing a new collar with a tinkling bell attached. 'My, oh, my, don't you look smart?' she said. 'Has Daddy been spoiling you?'

Lucas appeared in the doorway of the sitting room. 'He brought in a bird,' he said with a brooding glower.

'Oh… What type?'

'What does it matter what type?' he asked.

'Well,' she said as she hung up her coat, 'if it was a nightingale or a cuckoo I would probably be a little upset. But if it was a sparrow or a starling I wouldn't be as concerned.'

'We need to talk about what you plan to do with him when you leave,' he said. 'Are you planning to take him with you?'

Molly rolled her lips together for a moment. She could sense Lucas was in a tense mood. She wondered if he too was thinking of how quickly her time with him was passing. He hadn't said anything, but she had sensed the increased urgency in his lovemaking over the last few days. Was he thinking of how much he would miss her when she left? 'I hadn't really thought that far ahead…'

'Then you need to,' he said with a jarring brusqueness. 'I didn't sign up for cat ownership. I said I'd baby-sit him. I've done that. That's all I'm prepared to do.'

'So you'll kick him out when you kick me out, will you?'

His brows snapped together. 'I'm not kicking you out. You're here for a set time. We've both known that from the outset.'

Molly moved past him with a rolled-eye look. 'Whatever.'

'We've talked about this, Molly,' he said. 'You know the terms. I've never hidden them from you.'

She turned to face him. 'Why are you being so prickly this evening?' she asked. 'I came home all excited to tell you stuff about the dinner and you've done nothing but bite my head off since I walked through the door. Sometimes I think you don't really like having me here. I bet you're secretly counting the days until I leave.'

A long tense moment passed as his gaze tussled with hers. But then he expelled a breath and lifted a hand to rub the back of his neck. 'I'm sorry,' he said. 'I didn't mean to rain on your parade.' He dropped his hand back by his side. 'Tell me about your exciting news.'

Molly wasn't going to be won over that easily. 'You probably won't even find it exciting,' she said with a little pout. 'It's not like you really want a bunch of people—most of whom you won't know—wining and dining and dancing in your precious house. You probably only agreed to it to get me off your back.'

'I'm fine about it,' he said.

She gave him a cynical look.

'OK,' he conceded. 'It's not my idea of a fun night at home. But it's obviously important to you so I'm happy to go along with it.'

Molly gave him a haughty look and went to move up the stairs, but he stopped her with a hand on her wrist. 'Do you mind?' she said. 'I'm going upstairs to have a shower.'

His fingers tightened like a handcuff, and his eyes went dark, *very* dark as they locked on hers. 'Have one with me,' he said.

Molly felt a little shiver roll down her spine like a red-hot firecracker. Sparks of awareness prickled over her skin. Her breasts tightened beneath her clothes. Her legs trembled in anticipation of being thrust apart by his commanding possession. But some little demon of defiance pushed up her chin and ignited her eyes. 'What if I don't want to have one with you?' she said. 'What if I want to be on my own right now and sulk and brood and be in a rotten mood?'

He tugged her against him, thigh to thigh, hard male arousal to soft but insistent female need. 'Then I'll have to think of ways to convince you,' he said, and lowered his mouth to the sensitive skin of her neck.

Molly shivered again as she felt his teeth on her skin. It was a playful bite—the primal tug of an alpha male showing his selected mate that he meant business. She tilted her head as he moved down her neck to her left clavicle, his tongue moving over the tightly stretched skin, licking, laving and teasing. Her breasts tingled behind her bra as she felt his warm breath skate over her décolletage.

Sensual excitement sent her heart rate soaring as he pushed his hands up under her top to cup her breasts. His mouth sucked on the upper curve of her right breast pushed up by his hands. She snatched in a breath as she felt his teeth graze her flesh. He went lower, taking her lace-covered nipple in his mouth and sucking on it. It made her all the more desperate to feel his lips and tongue on her bare flesh.

She moved sinuously against him, rolling her hips against the proud jut of his erection, tantalising him with her body, wanting him to be as desperate for her as she was for him.

And he was.

He growled against her mouth as he finally covered it with his, thrusting his tongue through her parted lips to mate with hers in a heart-stopping tango. His hands worked at her clothes methodically but no less hastily. Molly did the same with his, but perhaps with a little less consideration for buttons and seams.

She had only just got him free of his trousers and underwear when he lowered her to the floor. The Persian rug tickled the skin of her back as she felt his weight come down over her. She gasped as he speared her with his body, a deep, bone-melting thrust that made her insides turn to molten lava. It was a frenzied coupling—rough, urgent, desperate and deliciously exciting. Her nerves shrieked in delight, twitching and tensing, contracting and convulsing as each deep thrust drove into her.

She started to climb to the summit. Up and up she went, her body stretching and stretching to reach that blissful goal. He increased his pace as if he had sensed her need for more friction. And then he brought his fingers into play against the swollen heart of her, tipping her over the edge into a tumultuous sea of mind-blowing sensations.

It went on and on, rolling waves coursing through her, each one sending another cataclysmic reaction through her body. She dug her fingers into his back, her teeth sinking into the skin of his shoulder as the riot of sensations shook and shuddered through her until she was finally spent. Still she hung onto him as he reached his own pinnacle of pleasure. She felt it power through her, an explosive release that had him slump against her once it was over.

Lucas eased himself away and offered her a hand to help her to her feet. 'About that shower,' he said. 'Have I convinced you to share it with me yet?'

Molly gave him a playful smile, her body still tingling from his passionate lovemaking. 'I don't know. What's in it for me?'

His eyes ran over her tousled form, leaving a trail of hot longing in their wake. 'You can't guess?'

Her insides fluttered with excitement. 'You're in a dangerous mood tonight, Dr Banning,' she said.

His mouth tilted upwards in a sexy half-smile, his eyes smouldering like hot coals. 'You'd better believe it, Dr Drummond,' he said, and scooped her up in his arms and carried her upstairs.

Molly was in a dangerous mood herself by the time Lucas had turned on the shower. She stepped into the cubicle with him, pushing against his chest with the flat of her hand until his back was up against the marbled wall of the shower. 'Stay,' she said, giving him a sultry look before she slithered down his body.

He gave a groan as she took him in her mouth. She felt his legs buckle and he thrust out a hand to brace himself as she worked on him. It was the most erotic thing she had ever done. She tasted the essence of him on her tongue as she swirled it over and around the head of his erection. He groaned again and she heard his breathing rate escalate. She felt the tension building in him; she could feel the blood surging through his veins, filling him, extending him to capacity and she drove him on relentlessly.

He tried to pull her away but she refused to budge. She drew on him, again and again, using the moistness of her mouth to lubricate him. She used her tongue again to tantalise him, to tease him, to take that final plunge. She felt the intimate explosion, felt the warm spill of his release, heard the raggedness of his breathing, felt the sag of his limbs as the pleasure flowed through him.

Molly got to her feet and rinsed her mouth under the flowing water before trailing her hands over his chest. 'Good?' she asked.

'Where the hell did you learn to do that?' he asked in a husky rasp.

'Instinct,' she said. 'You bring out the wild woman in me.'

He put his hands on her hips and brought her against him. 'You're incredible,' he said.

She turned in his arms and wiggled her behind against him. 'Scrub my back for me?'

He pumped a handful of shower gel from the dispenser on the wall and smoothed it over her back and shoulders. He used slow, stroking movements, caressing all the way down to the dip in her spine. She shuddered in pleasure as he trailed a finger down the crease of her bottom. She shifted her legs apart to give him better access and shuddered again when he found the swollen, pulsing heart of her. She gasped as he played with her, teasing her, taking her to the brink before backing off.

'Please...' Molly leant her weight against the shower wall in front of her. '*Oh, please...*'

'You like that?' he said as he brushed against her from behind.

She shivered as she felt his erection between her legs, every pore of her skin intensely aware of him. 'Yes, oh, yes,' she said.

He guided himself between her parted thighs, rubbing against her, letting her know he was about to mount her but letting her have full control. The sensation of him entering her from behind was wildly, wickedly erotic. There was a primitive aspect to it as he finally possessed her, his groin flush against her buttocks, his thighs braced around hers as he started thrusting, gently at first but slowly building momentum.

Molly was lost within seconds. She tumbled head-first into a whirlpool of such intense pleasure she was gasping and sobbing with it as it rumbled through her. The tight convulsions of her body triggered his release. She felt him pump himself empty, his hands holding her hips with a tight, almost fiercely possessive hold.

His whole body gave a shiver, and then he slowly turned her round and pushed her wet hair back off her face, his eyes dark and intense as they met hers. 'Still want to be on your own to sulk and brood?' he asked.

Molly put her hands on his chest and raised her mouth for his kiss. 'What do you think?'

CHAPTER ELEVEN

MOLLY DIDN'T KNOW if it was because she was so busy with work and organising the dinner dance that time felt like it was set on fast forward, but suddenly it was the day of the dance and she had only three weeks left of her post at St Patrick's.

She had taken the day before the event off to be at Lucas's house to help Gina with the final clean and polish before the flowers and decorations were delivered. The ballroom looked amazing by the time Saturday evening came around.

When Emma dropped by with the after-dinner chocolates a London chocolatier had donated, she gasped in wonderment when Molly led her in to see her handiwork. 'It's like something out of a fairy-tale,' she said turning around to look at the black and white helium-filled balloons festooned in giant bunches with satin ribbons dangling in curling tails.

'Uh-oh,' Molly said as Mittens made a grab for one of the ribbon tails. She scooped him up out of harm's way and hugged him close to her chest.

'Isn't he adorable?' Emma said, reaching to give him a pat.

'He's a little mischief maker, that's what he is,' Molly said. 'He's been unstoppable since he got his cast off.'

'Are you going to take him back with you to Sydney when you go?' Emma asked.

Molly felt the all too familiar pang seize her at the thought of leaving. She took Mittens to the entrance of the ballroom and closed the door to keep him out before she answered. 'I was hoping Lucas might keep him. But nothing's been decided as yet.'

Emma began to chew at her lower lip with her teeth. 'I was kind of hoping you and Lucas were going to stay together…' She looked at Molly and blushed. 'To be honest, I didn't feel like that at the beginning. I feel embarrassed about it now, but I think I was a bit in love with him myself. I suppose it was more of a crush really. But, then, I think a lot a patients fall in love with their doctors. My mum said she fell in love with her obstetrician, her GP *and* her dentist. I think falling in love with the dentist was taking it a bit far but anyway…'

Molly smiled wryly. 'I've had a few crushes over the years myself.'

'The thing is…' Emma continued. 'Dr Banning needs someone like you. You understand the stress and strain he's under because you experience it yourself. You probably think it's none of my business and I shouldn't be so impertinent to comment on your and his private life, but these last few weeks I feel I've got to know you. You love him, don't you?'

Molly gave her a bitter-sweet smile. 'Of course I do,' she said. 'But sometimes loving someone is not enough.'

'How can it not be enough?' Emma asked. 'Love is supposed to conquer all.'

'Lucas isn't ready to commit to a relationship,' Molly said. 'I can't force him to be ready. He has to do that in his own time.' *If he ever does*, she thought with a crippling pain around her heart.

'But he loves you,' Emma said. 'I know he does. It's so obvious. His eyes light up when you walk into the room. And he actually smiles now. He never used to do that before. It must be love.'

Molly wanted to believe her, but Emma was like a lot of young girls caught up in the romantic fantasy of seeing what she wanted to see.

Did Lucas love her?

She had thought so, but if he truly did why wouldn't he promise her the future with him she wanted so much?

Lucas had planned to help Molly with the preparations for the dinner dance but a new patient had come in with severe pancreatitis. He had been caught up with putting in a central line to the forty-eight-year-old man and managing his treatment. Time had slipped away, which it had a rather frightening habit of doing just lately.

As each day came to a close he felt a sickening feeling assail him. He would lie awake for hours with Molly asleep beside him, wondering how he was going to find the strength to let her go. He had thought about it from every angle but he always came to the same conclusion—she was better off without him.

He was concerned that she hadn't spoken to her father since that phone call when Jack Drummond had issued an ultimatum. He knew how much it distressed her to have to choose between him and her family. He had seen relatives torn apart with guilt when an estranged loved one was suddenly taken ill or, even worse, died without being reunited with their family. He couldn't bear to think of Molly having to live the rest of her life estranged from either one of her parents because of her involvement with him.

Her loyalty to him astounded him. And yet he couldn't quite shake the feeling that he didn't deserve it. He kept telling himself she would be better off with someone who didn't have a road train of baggage dragging behind, but every time he thought of her with someone else he felt like a lead boot was stomping on his chest.

Only that day one of the senior surgeons had playfully elbowed him in the ribs and told him to put a ring on Molly's finger before someone else did. Lucas had shrugged it off with an indifferent smile, but inside he'd been so knotted up he had scarcely been able to breathe.

How would he bear it? He'd already started to torture himself with how it might play out. He imagined how he would hear from one of his brothers that Molly had met some other guy—maybe another doctor—and was setting up a home and family with him. Maybe they would even send him photos of her wedding.

Dear God, how was he supposed to cope with that? His life had been pretty bleak before, but that would be taking it to a whole new level of misery.

He imagined the years passing… Molly would have a couple of kids, a little scrubby-kneed boy just like Matt and a gorgeous little sunny-faced princess like herself.

The children *he* wanted to have with her.

He swallowed against the prickly tide of despair that filled his throat. Why did life have to be so hard, *so cruel*? Hadn't he suffered enough, without life dumping more misery on his shoulders? He wanted to be normal again. How long ago that seemed! He had once been a normal kid with the same dreams and aspirations others had. Then fate had cut him from the herd and set him aside, marking him as different.

There was no chance of a normal life now. It would *never* be normal. He had to make the most of what he had and be grateful he had it, because so many—just like Matt—didn't even get the chance.

By the time Lucas came home from the hospital Molly was about to head upstairs to shower and dress for the dinner. He wished he could have spent the evening on his own with her rather than share her with a hundred or so people, but she was terribly excited about the money she and Emma were raising. He was proud of her. She had such a heart for people and the way she had mentored and supported Emma was a credit to her generous and giving nature.

'Sorry I'm so late,' Lucas said as he bent down to brush her lips with a kiss. 'I would've been back ages ago but I had trouble putting in a central line on my last patient. Anything I can do to help?'

She gave him a smile but he noticed it was a little shaky around the edges. 'No, it's all under control.' She crossed her fingers. 'I think.'

He suddenly realised she was nervous about this evening. 'Hey,' he said, tipping up her face. 'You've done a wonderful job. The house looks amazing. Tonight will be fabulous. Everyone is going to be super-impressed with your ability to put on a party to remember.'

Her grey-blue eyes looked misty all of a sudden. 'Lucas…' She blinked a couple of times and bit her lip and began to turn away. 'Never mind…'

He stalled her with a hand on her arm. 'No, tell me, what's worrying you?' he asked.

She looked up at him with a little frown pleating her forehead. 'I want this to be a wonderful night for you too,' she said. 'I want you to enjoy it, not just to endure it for my sake.'

Lucas cupped her face and looked deep into her gaze. 'If I can have the first and last dance and all the other ones in between with you then I will enjoy every single minute,' he said. 'Is it a deal?'

She smiled a smile that was like a blast of sunshine with just a few clouds floating around the edges. 'It's a deal.'

'Great party, Lucas,' Jacqui Hunter said as she scooped up a glass of fizzing champagne from a passing waiter. 'Your house is amazing. You really are a dark horse, aren't you? I didn't know you were such a DIY expert.'

Lucas gave a loose shrug as he took a sip of his soda water. 'It fills in the time.'

She waggled her brows at him. 'Seems to me you might need to find yourself another big old run-down mansion to spruce up in a few weeks,' she said. 'You could end up with a lot of time on your hands.'

He tried to ignore the jab of pain around his heart. 'Yeah, well, I've been looking around,' he said.

'Find anything?'

'Not much.'

'Didn't think so,' Jacqui said, glancing to where

Molly was smiling up at one of the single anaesthe-tists. 'A house like this is a once-in-a-lifetime sort of find, don't you think?'

Lucas put his glass down on a side table. 'Excuse me,' he said. 'I think someone's cutting in on my next dance.'

Molly smiled at him he approached. 'I thought you were going to stand me up,' she said. 'Tristan was going to fill in for you.'

Lucas gathered her up close and spun her away from the clot of other dancers. 'Yes, well, he can get to the back of the queue,' he said.

She gave him a teasing look. 'Are you jealous?'

He pretended to glower at her. 'When is this party going to be over?' he asked.

She gave him a crestfallen look. 'You're not enjoy-ing it, are you?'

He tapped her on the end of the nose with his finger. 'I'm enjoying seeing you enjoy yourself,' he said. 'It's a great party, not that I'm any judge. I can't remember the last time I went to one.'

She touched his face with the velvet soft caress of her palm. 'Maybe when it's over we can have a party of our own,' she said.

Lucas turned her out of the way of a rather enthusi-astic couple who hadn't quite figured out the timing on the waltz they were doing. 'Sounds like a good plan,' he said. 'Do I need to bring anything?'

She stepped up on tiptoe and brushed his ear with the soft vibration of her lips. 'Just you.'

Molly got the phone call just before coffee was served. She wouldn't have heard her phone at all if it hadn't been for Emma needing a sticky plaster for a blister she'd got while dancing with one of the handsome young residents from the hospital. She took Emma upstairs to the main bathroom and she heard her phone ringing in Lucas's room on her way back.

She told Emma to go on without her, and quickly picked up the phone, with the intention of ignoring the call if it wasn't the hospital or anyone important, but then she saw it was her mother. 'Mum? You're calling at an odd hour,' she said. 'Is everything all right?'

'Oh, darling,' her mother said. 'I have some terrible news.'

Molly felt an icy hand grasp at her heart. 'What's happened?'

'It's your father,' Margaret Drummond said. 'He and Crystal have been in an accident. He's OK apart from a broken ankle but Crystal has a ruptured placenta and—'

'Oh, God,' Molly gasped. 'What about the baby?'

Her mother was trying to talk through sobs. 'They had to do an emergency Caesarean. The baby's in the neonatal unit. They're not sure if he's going to make it. The priest has been in to christen him. Poor Crystal... it's just so awful. I don't know what to do.'

'Is she all right?' Molly asked. 'I mean physically?'

'They had to do a transfusion but, yes, she's out of danger now,' Margaret said. 'Your father is beside himself. Can you come home? I know I shouldn't ask you but I can't bear for you to be away at a time like this. Your father needs you right now. We all need you.'

'Of course I'll come,' Molly said, already rushing to her previous room where her suitcase was stored in one of the built-in wardrobes. 'I'll book a flight tonight. Try not to panic. I'll be there as soon as I can.'

Lucas appeared in the doorway a few minutes later just as Molly had turned on her laptop. 'What are you doing, checking emails now?' he said. 'I thought you promised me the last dance and then a private party?'

She clutched at her face with both hands. 'Oh, Lucas, I have to go home. I have to go right now.'

His brows came together. 'Whatever for?'

'My father and his wife were in an accident,' she said. 'Their baby had to be born via Caesarean, but he's so premature he might not make it. I have to go to help them. I can't be away from them at a time like this.'

'Of course you must go,' he said. 'Here, let me make the flight booking for you. You start packing. Just take the minimum. I'll send the rest of your stuff on later.'

Molly moved away from the computer and quickly changed into a travelling outfit. She started to pack, but she had barely tossed a change of clothes in the bag when she turned and looked at him. 'Please come with me,' she said. 'Take some leave from the hospital and come with me.'

Another frown—deeper this time—appeared between his brows. 'I can't leave.'

'Yes, you can,' Molly said. 'What if you were ill or something? They'd find someone else. I want you to come with me. I *need* you to come with me.'

He got up from the computer. 'I can't come with you, Molly,' he said.

Tears blurred her vision. 'That's because you don't *want* to come with me,' she said. 'You don't want to be with me—period. That's why you jumped at the chance to book my flight. You can't wait until I walk out that door for the very last time, can you?'

He went white with tension. 'That's not true,' he said. 'I'm merely trying to keep calm here. You're upset and not thinking straight.'

'Of course I'm upset!' Molly said. 'My father could've died tonight or tomorrow or whatever time it is there. Oh, God. I'll never forgive myself. I should've called him back. I shouldn't have been so stubborn. Now I might never get to meet my little brother.'

'Darling,' he said, and reached for her but she backed away.

'How can you call me that?' she asked. 'I'm not your darling. I'm just a fill-in, just like I was with Simon.'

'Now you really are talking rubbish,' he said in a steely tone.

'Am I?' she asked, challenging him with her gaze. 'Then come with me. Drop everything and come with me.'

A muscle beat like a maniacal hammer in his jaw. 'I will not be issued with ultimatums,' he said. 'That is no way to conduct a relationship.'

'Is that what we have—a relationship?' she asked. 'What we have is an arrangement. A housemates-with-benefits arrangement.'

'You know it's much more than that,' he said with a brooding look.

Molly gave a scornful snort as she flung another couple of things in her bag. 'Sure it is,' she said. 'That's why my stuff is still in this room instead of in your room with yours. And that's why you're not packing a bag right this minute and coming with me.'

'For God's sake, Molly, we have a hundred people downstairs,' he said through tight lips. 'Do you really expect me to drop everything and fly halfway around the world with less than five minutes' notice?'

Molly tried to see it from his perspective. It was a lot to ask at short notice. It was wrong to expect him to drop everything. She wouldn't like him to ask it of her if the tables were changed.

'You're right,' she said, releasing a breath. 'I'm sorry. I'm just all over the place with this.' She pinched the bridge of her nose, trying to keep her emotions under some semblance of control. 'What about in a few days' time?' She dropped her hand from her face to look at him again. 'Will you come then?'

His frown was heavy and forbidding. 'Molly…'

'What about early next week or the week after?' she asked. 'It will give you time to clear your diary, find a locum or someone to step in for you.' *Please, just say you'll try*, she silently begged.

His eyes moved away from hers. 'It's not that simple, Molly. I have patients, responsibilities. I have people depending on me.'

'But what about me?' Molly asked, trying to hold back tears. 'Aren't I important enough for you to put those responsibilities aside for just a few days to be with me when I need you most?'

He looked back at her again, but his expression was masked. 'Your flight leaves in a couple of hours,' he said. 'I've put you in business class so you can sleep.'

'But I can't afford to fly business class.'

'I've paid it for you.'

'I'll send you the money when I get home,' she said.

'Consider it a gift.'

Molly gave him a cynical look. 'A parting gift, Lucas?'

He thrust his hands in his trouser pockets, his expression still as blank as a brick wall. 'Are you coming back for the rest of your term?' he asked.

Molly closed her bag with a click that sounded like a punctuation mark being typed at the end of a sentence. 'You'll have to find someone else,' she said. 'I'll send you a formal resignation as soon as I get home.'

He gave a businesslike nod. 'Would you like me to drive you to the airport?'

I'd like you to tell me you love me, Molly thought as her heart gave a tight spasm. *I'd like you to tell me you can't bear the thought of me leaving. Tell me you love me. Tell me you can't live without me.* 'No, thank you,' she said. 'It'll be quicker if I just leave. I'm sorry to leave you with Mittens. I'll try and sort something out. I'm not sure what the quarantine arrangements are if I were to ship him home. It might be too stressful for him. Cats are funny like that. Maybe one of the nurses at the hospital will take him.'

'It's fine,' he said. 'He might get confused if he was taken somewhere else. This is his home now.'

'Right…well, I'd best get going, then,' Molly said. 'Will you give my apologies to everyone? I'm sure they'll understand it's an emergency.'

'Of course.' He looked at her then, his eyes dark and unreadable. 'Goodbye, Molly.'

Molly came up to him and going on tiptoe gently placed a soft kiss on his lean cologne-scented jaw. 'Goodbye, Lucas,' she said, and then she turned and walked out the door.

* * *

Lucas closed the front door as the last of the guests left. He looked at the emptiness of his house now that the party was over. It was like a big ship after a luxury cruise had ended or a kid's birthday party room after all the children had gone.

Empty.

Even the decorations looked exhausted. Some of the balloons looked as if they had let out a sigh of disappointment now that everyone had stopped playfully punching them about the dance floor. A black balloon bounced listlessly across the floor towards his foot. He gave it a half-hearted kick and let out a string of curses his mother would have washed his mouth out for when he was a kid.

Mittens came mewing through the house. He had stayed away while the party was in full swing. He gave Lucas a quizzical look and peered around as if looking for Molly.

'She's gone,' Lucas said, bending down to pick him up. He held him against his chest and stroked his velvety head.

'Prrrput?' Mittens said, and head-bumped his hand.

Lucas blinked to clear his vision but still the tears kept coming as if a tap had been turned on somewhere deep inside him. 'You're right,' he said. 'This place sucks without her.'

CHAPTER TWELVE

'YOU'RE *ACTUALLY GOING* on leave?' Jacqui asked, swinging round to face Lucas in the office a week later.

Lucas took off his stethoscope and dropped it on the desk. 'Why are you so surprised?' he asked. 'I'm entitled to some time off, aren't I?'

'Well, yes, of course, but you haven't even taken sick leave in I don't know how long,' she said. 'Where are you going?'

'Nowhere special.'

Jacqui folded her arms as she leaned her hips back against the desk. 'So it's finally happened.'

He shot her a quick sideways look as he straightened the papers on the desk. 'What's finally happened?'

'You're finally ready to go home.'

Was he ready?

No, not really. It was a hurdle he had to face—a bridge to cross. He wasn't sure of his reception on the other side but he couldn't waste another moment worrying about it. He wanted to be where Molly was, tell her how much he loved her, how he couldn't bear the thought of the rest of his life without her in it, making him smile, making him feel loved, making him *live* again.

How had he thought he could survive without her? This past week had been one of the loneliest weeks of his life. Even Mittens had joined him in his misery by moping about as if the sun was never going to come out again.

Molly was his sunshine, his only light in the darkness of what his life had become.

She was his second chance, his *only* chance.

'I have a little favour to ask you,' Lucas said.

'Sure,' Jacqui said, eyes twinkling. 'What is it?'

'Do you know anything about cats?'

'He's beautiful,' Molly said as she looked at little baby Oliver Matthew Drummond lying in the neonatal crib.

Jack Drummond brushed at his eyes with his hand, carefully juggling his crutches to do so. 'Yeah, he is,' he said. 'You were too. You were the prettiest baby in the nursery. I felt so proud. Scared out of my wits, though.'

Molly gave him a quizzical look. 'Scared? Why?'

'There weren't a lot of females about the place while I was growing up,' he said. 'Your gran died when I was twelve. Dad had to do things pretty rough and ready, bringing up four boys on his own. Having a daughter terrified me. I guess that's why I left a lot of it up to your mother. I knew how to handle a son because I'd been one myself and I'd had little brothers to help rear. But a little girl dressed in pink? Well, I guess I didn't always get it right with you, did I?'

Molly was still not ready to forgive him. 'No, you didn't.'

He cleared his throat, looking exactly what he was—a rough-and-tumble country man, out of his depth with showing emotion or even witnessing it in others. 'Thanks for coming, love. I reckon the little tyke held on just so he could meet his big sister. The doctors reckon he's out of danger now.'

'I'm happy for you and Crystal,' she said. 'I really am.'

He cleared his throat again. 'Yeah, well, I wanted to talk to you about things.' He let out a long breath. 'I'm a stubborn old goat. Your mother will tell you that— Crystal too, if it comes to that. I wish I'd handled things differently. Not just with the divorce but just…things…'

'You were wrong about Lucas,' she said, looking at the sleeping baby again. 'You were *so* wrong.'

'I know,' he said. 'I've been wanting to talk to you about that all week.'

Molly turned and looked at him again with tears springing into her eyes. 'I love him, Dad. I'm not going to apologise for it. He's the most wonderful man I've ever met. He's suffered so much for what happened with Matt. It wasn't his fault. You know it wasn't. I can't bear to think of him over there all alone. He just works, that's all he does. He works and works and works. He has no life. I *want* him to have a life. I want a life with him. I know it will be hard for you, but I can't live without him. I don't want to live without him.'

'I never really thought of how it was for him until I saw that car suddenly veer in front of me,' Jack said. 'It must have been like that for him when he rounded that bend and that roo jumped out in front of him. In that split second you don't have time to think. You just react. He was a young, inexperienced driver. He did what any young driver would do. It wasn't his fault.'

'Do you really mean that?' she asked.

He looked at Molly with red-rimmed eyes, his throat moving up and down like a tractor piston. 'It wasn't his fault. I want to tell him that. I know it's seventeen years too late, but I want to call him and tell him that. Do you have his number?'

Molly couldn't control the wobble of her chin. Her eyes were streaming and her throat felt raw with emotion but she thought she had never loved her father more than at that point. 'Of course I have his number,' she said. 'Let's go to the relatives' room so it'll be more private.'

Jack handed back her phone a few minutes later. 'He's not answering,' he said. 'I would've left a message but I'd rather speak to him person to person.'

Molly checked her watch. 'He's probably still at the hospital. He works the most ridiculous hours. I told you he was a workaholic.' She looked up at her father and frowned when she saw his expression. 'What?'

Jack gave a crooked smile. 'I wouldn't want him to come anywhere near my little girl if he wasn't dedicated and responsible. He saves lives, Molly. What could be more important than that?'

Molly blew out a breath. 'I'll try the hospital,' she said, and scrolled down for the number. 'If he's not there then I haven't got a clue where else he would be.'

She hung up the phone half a minute later. 'He's on leave.'

'Where?'

'No one knows,' she said. 'He didn't say but, then, he wouldn't. He never tells anyone anything.'

'I'd better get back to Crystal,' Jack said. 'You'll let me know if you hear from him?'

Molly's shoulders dropped on a sigh. 'Yes, but don't hold your breath.'

Lucas breathed in a lungful of hot air as he walked out of Mascot airport. He couldn't get over the Australian accents surrounding him. Even the airport announcements had sounded exaggerated, as if the person on the loudspeaker was pretending to be an Aussie. He hadn't realised his accent had changed until he'd jumped in a taxi and the guy had asked him if it was his first time visiting the country. His brothers had been ribbing him about it for years but now he realised he was one of those ex-pats who didn't really know where they belonged any more.

He checked through his messages as he headed to the taxi rank. There were dozens from the hospital but that wasn't unusual. It was probably hard for the staff to get it into their heads that he was actually on leave.

There was one message he was particularly thrilled about, however. Tim's latest scan had shown some definite activity and his mother had felt his fingers curl around hers when she spoke to him. It was just the sort of response he had been hoping for. The recovery might be slow but he was hopeful it would be like Emma's.

There was a missed call from Molly's phone but no message. He wasn't sure what to make of that. Maybe she had just wanted to let him know she had got home safely.

He headed straight to the private hospital in the eastern suburbs. He had done a quick phone around to track down Molly and her family. It really helped, being part of the medical profession. One of the guys he'd worked with at St Patrick's was now a neonatal specialist at Sydney Metropolitan. He had given Lucas an update on Molly's little half-brother. The little guy was out of danger now. That was great news but Lucas still wasn't sure how he would be received, turning up in the middle of a family crisis. But he couldn't stay away. He wanted to be with Molly, not just now but always. How could he have thought otherwise? His life without her was like his house without a party or a cruise ship without passengers.

Empty.

It was weird, walking into a hospital from the other side of the counter, so to speak. He was just a visitor here, not one of the top specialists. An officious nurse gave him directions to the neonatal ward. Lucas assumed Molly would be somewhere near her little brother.

And he was right.

He saw her from a way off. She was standing outside the unit, looking in through the glass window.

But she wasn't alone.

Lucas stopped in his tracks. He didn't want to cause a scene in the middle of the neonatal unit. But neither did he want to slink away as if he was scared to stand up to Jack Drummond. But before he could take a step forwards or backwards Jack turned and saw him.

'Lucas?'

Molly swung around and her mouth dropped open. *'Lucas?'*

'Did you call me?' Lucas said. It was the first thing

that came into his head. There were a thousand things that he should have said instead but it was all he could think of at the time. It was so good to see her. She looked gorgeous. Tired, but gorgeous. She was dressed in tight-fitting jeans and a loose jersey top that had slipped off one of her shoulders. He wanted to crush her to him, feel that soft little body against his hard one and never let her go.

'What are you doing here?' Molly asked.

'I came to see you,' he said. 'To tell you I love you.'

Her eyes widened to the size of dinner plates. 'You came all that way to tell me that?' she said. 'Why didn't you tell me the night of the party?'

'I was an idiot that night,' Lucas said. 'I was caught off guard. I'd worked myself up to you leaving in another three weeks. I wasn't prepared for you to just up and go like that.'

'Can I say something here?' Jack stepped forward. '*Dad.*'

'No, let me speak,' Jack said. He turned to Lucas. 'I was wrong to blame you for Matt's death. I don't expect you to forgive me. I'll never forgive myself. You were like another son to Margie and me. I can't believe I treated you the way I did. For all these years I've blamed you for something that was never your fault.

'I just want you to know that I'm sorry. It's too late to undo the damage I did to Margie. How she still speaks to me is testament to the sort of person she is. But I don't want Molly to suffer any more. She's just like her mother—loving and generous to a fault. I want her to be happy. I think you're the only person who can make her so.'

'Can I have a word with you in private?' Lucas said to Jack. 'There's something I want to ask you.'

Molly put her hands on her hips. 'Excuse me?' she said. 'Hello? Don't I have some say in this?'

Jack grinned from ear to ear as he slapped Lucas on the shoulder. 'She's all yours, mate,' he said. 'She'll drive you nuts and make you tear your hair out at times, but she'll stick with you through thick and thin. She's a good girl. I'm proud of her. I'm proud of you, too. You're a good man. I'll be proud as punch to call you my son-in-law.'

Molly glowered at her father. 'Dad, you're jumping the gun here. He hasn't even asked me.'

'I'm getting to it,' Lucas said with a melting look. 'But you know me, darling, I don't like being rushed.'

Molly felt her heart give a little flip like a pancake, but she still wasn't going to capitulate without a show of spirit. 'You're assuming, of course, that I will say yes?' she said with a pouting, you-hurt-me-and-I'm-not-quite-ready-to-forgive-you look. 'I've been crying myself to sleep for the past week. You didn't even send me a text.'

'I know,' Lucas said. 'I just couldn't say what I wanted to say in a text. I wanted to see you.' He brought her up close, his arms wrapping around her securely. 'Will you marry me, Molly? I want you to be my wife. I want you to be the mother of my babies. I want to spend the rest of my life with you. I want to love you, laugh with you, fight with you, celebrate and commiserate with you. I even want to party with you. I want to live life with you no matter what it dishes up. I just want to be with you.'

'For God's sake, Molly, put the poor man out of his misery,' Jack said.

Molly smiled as she flung her arms around Lucas's neck. 'Yes,' she said. 'Yes, yes, yes, a thousand million squillion times yes.'

Lucas laughed as he swung her around in his arms. It was the first time he had laughed since he'd been a teenager. It felt good. It felt really good.

It felt right.

* * * * *